NEVER YOUR LADY

NEVER YOUR LADY

CLAY WADE – BOOK 4

ART CLEPPER

NEVER YOUR LADY
CLAY WADE - BOOK 4

ISBN: 979-8-9858682-0-3 (sc)
ISBN: 979-8-9858682-1-0 (e)

CHAPTER ONE

The heat was stifling. Sweat ran down his face burning his eyes and blurring his vision while mosquitos and flies added to his misery. His horses stood twenty feet away stamping their feet and swishing their tails. He was still lying where he stopped rolling when he dived off his horse. Knowing movement attracts the eye he remained perfectly still. His pistol was in front of his face with the hammer pulled back to full cock, and he had no idea when it got there. The only thing moving was his eyes, darting from side to side, to detect any movement. His heart was beating as if he had just run a mile. He watched his horses out of the corner of his eye for any reaction, knowing they would see or hear movement long before he would. So far, they had not indicated anyone else was around. But Clay knew different.

He had just leaned to his left to check the trail he was following when the arrow came out of nowhere and missed him by inches. If he had not leaned when he did it would have gone into his chest.

The spot where he laid was more open than he liked, but that's the hand he was dealt, and he would have to play it out. There was no raise or call in this game. If you win you live, if you lose, you die.

Four days ago, he left his home near Cuero, Texas, in a race to save his son's life. He was assuming the culprits were Apaches, but he was only guessing. No one had seen anything. When Carter didn't come for supper when called, Clay went looking. Carter was supposed to be fishing down at the creek that ran at the bottom of the hill a half-mile from the house. Clay found Carter's fishing pole lying on the ground, and two nice size fish on a stringer, but no sign of Carter. Clay called several times but got no answer. He knew immediately something was wrong. Carter was too disciplined and dependable to wander off without telling someone where he was going, and he would never have wandered off and left his catch here. Clay began searching for signs. He found where a scuffle took place about twenty yards from the fishing pole, and moccasin prints mixed with Carter's boot prints. His heart skipped a couple of beats, and he said a silent prayer that this wasn't what it looked like. Ten years of living here without a sign of Indian trouble, and now this.

He followed the tracks from the creek to a grove of trees a short distance away. There he found tracks where at least six horses had recently stood. The tracks led off to the north, staying behind the grove of trees, which kept them out of sight from the house and barns.

Clay followed the tracks for a quarter-mile and saw they continued out of sight. He could see for almost a mile, and there was no sign of anyone. He hurried back to the house and informed Marilyn and Lefty, who was the only man around at that time. All the other men were out on the range somewhere. Marilyn saw him running toward the house and knew something was wrong. She met him at the door with a worried look and a question on her face. She didn't get a chance to ask before Clay told her what he had found. He asked her to put together a bag of food and get his guns together while he saddled his horse.

When he came out of the house Lefty had Clay's horse saddled and another one for himself.

Clay asked, "What are you doing?"

"I'm going with you. You said there are at least six of them. This ain't gonna be no picnic, and they already have several hours head start on you."

"Yes, I know, but I would like you to be here in case they, or their friends, decide to come back. I don't want to leave the women and children here alone."

"But what can you do by yourself when you catch up to them?"

"I'll have to figure that out when I catch them."

"You better take an extra horse. You can travel faster and trade-off and not tire them out so much."

"Ok, how about I take this one since you won't need it?

Lefty removed his saddle and Clay hurried back to the house where Marilyn had his rifle, his extra pistol, holster, and a hundred rounds of ammunition laid out for him. She handed him his cartridge belt with his knife in the scabbard, along with a bag of beef jerky, coffee, coffee pot, skillet, and a small bag of salt in a sack that he tied onto his saddle. Knowing he was in a desperate hurry to get on the trail of the kidnappers, she didn't take up much of his time. She threw her arms around his neck and kissed him, stepped back, and said, "Hurry, Clay, be careful, and bring our son back safe." There were tears in her eyes, and her lip trembled, but she held herself together until Clay was out of sight, then she broke down and cried uncontrollably.

Clay took up their trail and followed it at a gallop until it was almost too dark to see their tracks, but six horses traveling at a gallop left a pretty good trail. Every so often, he slowed to a walk to give the horses a brief breather. The tracks did not deviate much from the straight line they were on.

The sun went down and the moon hadn't come out yet and it was too dark to see the tracks. Clay was taking a chance that they continued on the same course.

A couple of hours later, the moon came up bright in a clear sky full of stars making it almost as bright as day. He slowed again to check for their tracks. He didn't see any signs where they had come this way, so thinking he had just strayed off their trail, he took a ninety-degree turn to the left and continued walking his horse, looking for their tracks. After a half-mile and not finding any sign, he turned back and went the other direction for a half-mile or so. He still didn't find the trail. He was getting more and more anxious and frustrated as the minutes flew by. They must have changed directions while it was too dark for him to see their tracks.

He turned back, retracing his tracks. It took him almost an hour to find where they turned in a more westerly direction.

Clay knew from his previous trip through west Texas that there was virtually nothing between here and Mexico. If he didn't overtake them before they crossed the border, Carter was going to be in deep, deep trouble, and finding him and getting him back was going to be much more difficult. Not only would he have the Indians to contend with, but also the Mexican military and the roving Mexican bandits. He had heard they could be as bad, or worse, to deal with as the Indians.

He picked up the speed and had no trouble following the trail now that the moon and stars were out so bright.

All through the night, he rode, stopping only occasionally to rest his horses. He kept looking ahead, hoping to see a fire or some indication that they had stopped for the night, but by the time the sun was coming up the next morning, there was no sign that they had stopped for anything. Their tracks were still there in front of him. He was so tired he could hardly keep his eyes open, and the horses were worn out. They had been traveling, with only short breaks from time to time, for over twelve hours.

He was looking for a likely place to stop when he spotted a line of trees at the bottom of a hill.

"We'll, boys, that looks like we may find some water and shade down there. What do you say we check it out?"

The tracks he was following took a turn and headed in that direction. He pulled up in a hurry and moved behind a large mesquite bush and pulled his binoculars from his saddlebag. He took a careful look around in all directions, then dismounted and squatted down to get a more stable stance to steady his binoculars and focused on the line of trees. His horses stamped their feet and pulled on the reins. They smelled water and were impatient to get to it. After several minutes of searching, he saw no signs of anyone. He spent a few more minutes checking out the area. When he still didn't see anything, he mounted his horse, pulled his rifle from the scabbard under his right leg, jacked a round into the barrel and with the butt resting on his right thigh, slowly approached the trees. He stopped several times to survey the area. When he finally arrived at the edge of the water, there were plenty of signs that the Indians had been here. There was no sign of a fire or any place where anyone laid down to rest. It was just a short stop for water.

He scouted the area looking for some sign of Carter. All he found was a few prints made by a boot like the ones Carter wore. The Indians were all wearing moccasins, so Carter's tracks were easy to spot.

CHAPTER TWO

When he was sure the Indians had left the area, he unsaddled his horses and led them to water, gave each of them a brief rubdown, and staked them on a patch of grass near the stream where they could eat and drink. As soon as he walked away, both horses lay down and rolled until they were covered with mud where the dirt mixed with their sweat. When they were satisfied, they stood and shook like a dog coming out of water. He got the bag of food Marilyn had fixed for him and settled down for a brief rest. He had not eaten anything since noon yesterday and didn't realize how hungry he was until he took the first bite. He thought his stomach was going to rebel at the sudden intrusion. He only intended to give himself and the horses a two-hour rest. He sat leaning against a tree eating and drinking water from his canteen.

As worried as he was about Carter, he didn't think he would get much rest. He was anxious to get going, but the horses needed rest. He was more tired than he thought. When he awoke, the sun was straight overhead. He jumped up and cursed himself for falling asleep when Carter was depending on him. He quickly saddled his horse and repacked his supplies, filled his canteen, and hit the trail again.

He was frustrated with himself for sleeping so long and letting them get farther ahead.

He pushed his horses harder, trying to make up the time he lost. He changed horses about every two hours, and using his hat, gave them a drink of water from his canteen.

All-day long he pushed his horses hard, desperate to catch up with whoever had his son.

When the sun was low in the sky and shining directly in his eyes and making it hard to see what was in front of him, he stopped to give his horses a short rest and let the sun get behind the horizon.

He dismounted and removed the saddle and put it on the other horse and cinched it up. He could see the tracks still out in front of him, and they were still going almost due west. He found a shaded place behind a mesquite bush, and with his gun belt and holster rolled into a ball for a pillow, he stretched out on the hot ground. It felt so good just to be out of the saddle, but as hard as he tried, he couldn't relax. All he could think about was what Carter was going through. He forced himself to be patient and give the horses time to rest while the sun got lower in the sky.

When he estimated thirty minutes had passed, he raised his head to check the sun. It was low enough now that he was not blinded by it, so he got up, brushed the dirt off his clothes, slung the gun belt around his hips, and buckled it. He gave each horse another sip of water, spoke softly to them, and mounted up and headed out.

With the sun down and the stars coming out, he had no trouble following the trail. He put his horse in a slow lope and let him go until he showed signs of tiring, and then he switched the saddle to his other horse and continued.

He rode until he figured it must be past midnight when he stopped and unsaddled his horse and staked them where they could feed on what little grass and brush they could find. After giving each of them another sip of water, he stretched out on the ground and was asleep almost immediately. But then the dreams started.

Indians were attacking the ranch. Ellen, his first wife, and Carter's mother, who was killed in a freak accident, was lying on the ground with blood on her head. Carter was missing, and Marilyn was fighting beside him, holding their baby daughter.

The dream was a jumble of things that made no sense, and he awoke, breathing hard and covered with sweat. He sat up and ran his hand across his face and looked around. Then it all came back to him: Where he was and what he was doing there. He checked the position of the moon and determined it would be daylight in another hour, so he got up, saddled his horse while chewing on a stick of jerky. Before riding out, he gave each horse another sip of water. The water in the canteen was getting too low for comfort. He remembered the last time he came through here they almost died of thirst while he was running from the haunting memories of Ellen's death. That was seven years ago. But with all that has happened since then, that seemed like a lifetime. This time he was depending on the Indians to lead him to water. They have lived in this country for hundreds, maybe thousands of years, and know the location of all the water holes. He was counting on that. So far, they had only stopped that one time. That was over twenty-four hours ago. They either knew where they could find the next water, or they had some big water bags. Either way, he was hoping they would lead him to water very soon. He and his horses were beginning to suffer from their short rations. He could get by on a cup of water every few hours, but the horses needed a lot more than that to keep going.

For two more days, he followed their trail. And like he was hoping they would, they led him to water at least once a day. He saw where they watered their horses and filled their water bags and where they laid on their belly to drink. At each stop, he was able to find Carter's tracks. He was walking on his own and didn't appear to be tied, or confined in any way. Clay couldn't tell if he was riding with one of the Indians, or had a horse to himself. He was an excellent rider for a nine-year-old, and he was smart when it came to taking care of his own needs, so he probably wasn't giving them much trouble. Indians were known for taking in young children and raising them like their own. So, as long as Carter didn't give them too much trouble, they probably wouldn't hurt him. Clay was hoping and praying Carter was smart enough to realize that. In the past, he had not shown any signs of getting scared or panicked easily.

Clay was remembering a time at the branding pens when Carter got off his horse for something, and a bull charged him.

Carter calmly stepped behind a post, and the bull went by on one side while Carter dodged to the other. The bull made several passes at Carter, but he was much more agile than the bull and could move around the post faster. That went on for what seemed like a very long time but was less than a minute until the bull gave up and trotted off. Carter was laughing and watched him until he was a safe distance away, then walked over and mounted his horse. Carter looked around at Clay, laughing, and said, "That was fun."

At each stop, Clay filled his canteens and allowed his horses to drink their fill, and then he drank from his canteen and refilled it again.

He had just reached the last water hole the Indians had led him to and decided to rest here until the moon came out. The sun had just gone down so it would be two or three hours at least before the night was light enough to see their trail.

From the tracks left by the Indians' horses, they didn't appear to be pushing them as hard now. They just seldom stopped for anything.

Clay had heard stories of Indians riding their horses until they dropped and then eat them. He had not seen any dead horses yet.

He rested and drank water until he felt like he would float away. The moon finally came up and lit up the countryside enough that he could follow the trail fairly quickly. He took his time to make sure he didn't lose them. When he was farther away from the water, it was easier to distinguish their tracks from the other animals that had come to drink. He picked up his pace and continued at an easy gallop and held that until his horses slowed on their own. He switched his saddle to his other horse and continued. When the second horse began to slow, he stopped for the rest of the night. There was nothing as far as he could see except scrub brush and a few cactus and sage.

He stopped and threw his saddle and blanket on the ground, watered his horses, and staked them so they wouldn't wander off. There was nothing for them to eat, but they would get some rest. He took his binoculars, and even though it was dark, he scanned the area to see if he could spot anything that might be a danger. He was primarily looking for a campfire. After several minutes of searching and not seeing anything, he stretched out on his blanket, using his saddle for a pillow, and chewed on a stick of jerky until he dozed off to the sound of coyotes barking in the distance.

CHAPTER THREE

As usual, it was a restless sleep filled with wild dreams and reliving the past. Some of his dreams were so real it took a while to figure out where he was when he awoke.

He checked on his horses and saw them standing with heads down sleeping as horses do.

He lay back down and tried to sleep but memories kept interfering. He was fighting in the war, was injured, and ended up in a union hospital in Richmond, Virginia. He was still there when the war ended. When he finally made his way home he discovered he had been reported killed in action, his family had died, his fiancée married to another man, thinking he was dead. Carpetbaggers had taken over the family farm and laid claim to all the livestock, which consisted of over four hundred head of cattle, and twenty-something horses. He recruited a few friends and rounded up the horses and cattle and drove them to market. During all of that, he fell in love with a neighbor's daughter, married her, moved to Texas, and started over. Three years later, Ellen, his wife, was killed in a freak accident, leaving him with a two-year-old son. The shock of losing her was too much, so in the dead of night, he saddled his horses and disappeared.

(A Lost Man, book 3.}

For five years he roamed, grieving over his loss, not caring if he lived or died until he found Marilyn.

He was acting as a deputy sheriff tracking a gang of bank robbers when he found Marilyn and her family being held captive by the outlaws. That turned his life around and he found a new reason for living. They were married and returned to his ranch near Cuero, Texas to settle down and raise their family.

Their new baby was only a few months old when Carter was taken by Indians and turned his life into another hell.

He awoke drenched in sweat, breathing hard and disoriented.

The next day was like the days before until mid-afternoon. The sun was burning the shirt off his back, and the glare from the ground and sky was so bright he could hardly see when he stopped for a brief rest. He dismounted and switched his saddle to his second horse. As he lifted his canteen to his mouth to take a drink, his eyes picked up a small dust cloud ahead. He froze with the canteen halfway to his mouth. He studied the dust for a few minutes and determined it could only be a couple of miles ahead. He was standing out there in a wide-open desert with only cactus and a mesquite bush to hide him if anyone should look this way. He led his horses behind the nearest bush to conceal them as much as possible. He would be surprised if the Indians had binoculars, but they were supposed to have excellent eyesight, and they knew this country much better than he did. He had to be extra careful from here on. If he could see their dust, then they would be able to see his. After a brief rest, which was hard for him to do now that he was this close, he mounted his horse and continued at an easy walk trying not to stir up dust that would let them know he was coming. He wanted to slap the spurs to his horse and go charging ahead with guns blazing and leave all of them dead. But common sense told him that would get him killed and leave Carter to live the life of an Indian.

He forced himself to remain calm and think about what he could do when he caught up with them. All he could do now was stay on their trail until they stopped somewhere. Maybe then he would have a chance to sneak in and steal Carter away.

The rest of the afternoon seemed like an eternity. He moved at a steady walk, and tried to stay behind some type of cover as he followed. Moving from one bush, or tree, which were few and far between, was increasing the distance he was traveling, but it was the best he could do to stay out of sight from anyone who may be watching their back trail.

The shadows grew long, and the sun was shining directly in his face again, making it difficult to see anything in front of him. He stopped behind a bush to conceal himself as much as possible until the sun got lower in the sky. He took advantage of the stop to rest his horses and himself for a few minutes. Now that he was this close it was almost impossible to force himself to stop. When the sun finally disappeared behind the mountain, he took his binoculars and searched the terrain before him. The dust was still there. He couldn't afford to get too close until after nightfall, so he took his time following and keeping the dust in sight until it was too dark to see.

The temperature dropped quickly when the sun went down, but it was still warm. It had been so hot during the day that it now felt almost cool.

If they followed their usual pattern, they would not stop for the night unless they came to water.

Even though it was too dark to see more than a few feet, Clay continued, depending on his horses to let him know if anything was close. The moon came up an hour or so later and lit the plains we'll enough for him to see their tracks.

It must have been close to midnight, and he was ready to stop for the night when he saw the flicker of a fire ahead. With his binoculars, he could make out the shapes of men moving around the fire. He tried desperately to get a glimpse of Carter, but he was too far away to distinguish one figure from the other.

He tried to determine the direction of the wind so he could stay crosswind from them. He didn't want the horses to catch the scent of each other and give his presence away, but the night was so still he couldn't feel any movement at all.

The fire appeared to be a couple of miles away, but at night distances can be deceiving. He mounted his horse and proceeded at a slow walk. After he had gone, what he considered was a mile, and the fire was still some distance off, he moved off the trail and staked his horses in a clump of brush. He looked around to get the landmarks and location firmly engraved in his mind so he could find them later. He didn't tie them so tight that they couldn't get themselves loose if they tried hard enough. He didn't want them left here to starve if he didn't make it back.

He took a long drink from his canteen and hung it back on his saddle. He took his rifle, removed his boots and spurs, stuffed them in the saddlebags, and put on his moccasins. After taking another good look around to make sure he could find his horses when he returned, he proceeded toward the fire on foot. He circled to the south to come upon the fire from that direction in case they had someone watching their back trail. After an hour of carefully sneaking through the brush, he was within a hundred yards of the fire. He saw nothing moving and assumed they were all sleeping. Even with his binoculars, he couldn't see any movement. He looked for their horses but couldn't see them either. He needed to know where they were so he wouldn't come upon them suddenly and cause them to set off the alarm. He made a complete circle around the camp but still didn't find the horses. He got a sick feeling in his stomach, knowing something had gone wrong. After searching the camp again with his binoculars, and seeing nothing but the fire, he slowly approached until he was standing just out of reach of the dim light of the fire. Apparently, they only stopped for a brief rest, food, and water and moved on, leaving the fire burning. He got that sick feeling in his stomach again. Did they know he was following them and left the fire burning to fool him?

He stomped the ground and cursed himself for letting them get away after he was so close. But since he was there, he looked the camp over for any signs of Carter. He found the same small boot tracks and a place where he had laid down to rest. Again it looked as if he were doing everything on his own and didn't appear to be tied or roughed up. Clay could only hope he was right.

It took him a half-hour to get back to his horses and get on the trail again. By then, he was so tired he could hardly stay in the saddle, but he forced himself to continue long into the night.

When he became aware of his surroundings again, it was almost daylight, and he had been following their trail all night. He was staying in the saddle by instinct and habit. He must have been sleeping for some time, for the terrain had changed from open desert with a few cactus, mesquite, and cedar, to thick brush with hardly a trail through it. He stopped to get his bearings and realized he could have ridden up on them and gotten himself killed and would never have known it. He had to stop for a while and get some rest and rest his horses. He leaned to his left to see if their tracks were still there when an arrow flew by so close, if he had still been upright in the saddle, it would have gone into his chest. He threw himself to the ground, drawing his pistol as he went down. He rolled and scooted another twenty feet or so before he came to a stop. He lost his hat in the scramble, but that was the least of his worries right now.

Although it was still early morning, the temperature had to be over ninety degrees, and there was no breeze stirring. It was stiflingly hot, sweat was running into his eyes, and he was afraid to move to wipe it away.

After what seemed like a very long time, he started slowly moving away from his horses, thinking if anyone were trying to sneak up on him, they would be watching the horses. He worked his way deeper into the thicker brush. No one was going to get close to him without the horses knowing about it. He could only hope they didn't spot him and put an arrow in him before he saw them.

He moved as slow as a snail, trying his best to make no noise, which was hard to do since he was lying in a bed of dry leaves and dead branches that had fallen from the thorny bushes that surrounded him.

After a long time, and no new holes in his body, he felt a little safer. He was in very thick cover and felt less exposed. His horses were fifty feet away, but he had a good view of them. He waited while nothing happened. It got even hotter if that was possible.

One of his horses, and then the other, raised his head with his ears pricked forward and looked in Clay's direction, but behind him. Something was moving back there, and he couldn't see it, or get a shot at it without moving, and that would give his position away if they didn't know where he was already. He was expecting an arrow or bullet in the back at any moment. He tensed and was on the verge of rolling over when he saw a movement out of the corner of his eye by his horses. The horses were looking in that direction also. He could only hope there were only two of them. If he moved to get one, he was going to expose himself to the second one and stand a good chance of getting killed.

He waited to see what the one by the horses was going to do. Clay was watching him and listening for any movement that would tell him if there were more of them around.

With the sweat running down his face into his eyes, blurring his vision, and flies swarming around his face, he was having a hard time keeping his eyes open. All he could do was blink. He moved his head slightly to get a better look toward the horses and saw an Indian slowly creeping through the brush toward them. His back was turned somewhat toward Clay as he was looking toward the horses. With the Indian's attention on the horses, Clay slowly turned his head to look the other way. The brush was so thick he could only see a few feet except right at the ground. For a foot or so up from the ground, the brush was not so thick. Clay cut his eyes as far as he could without moving his body. He was just turning back when he saw something move to his left rear about twenty feet away. He watched until it moved again. It was a moccasin from the knee down. So now he had two located, one on his right near the horses, another on his left rear. He slowly turned his head, scanning the ground as far as he could see from left to right. The one closer to the horses was looking around, trying to find Clay. It wasn't going to be too many more seconds until he spotted him, so Clay slowly swung his pistol to get it in line for a shot.

The Indian must have seen the movement and turned his head and looked Clay square in the eye. Clay's gun was pointed directly at him while the Indian's bow and arrow were pointed in the other direction. A look of fear flashed through the Indian's eyes as he tried to bring his weapon around for a shot, knowing he wasn't going to make it, but he had to try. Clay pulled the trigger and saw the Indian stagger back and grab his chest. With a look of pure hatred in his eyes, he tried to bring his bow up, but didn't have the strength and slowly crumpled to the ground. Clay was already turning back to his left when the second Indian came charging through the brush. He didn't know where Clay was and almost ran over him before Clay stopped him with a bullet to the head. He went down and was dead before he hit the ground. Clay quickly looked around to see if there were any more. When he didn't see or hear anything, he breathed a sigh of relief but didn't move from his position. After waiting another thirty minutes, watching his horses for any sign of movement, and they didn't indicate anyone else was around; he slowly rose from the ground and moved to stand between his horses. He wiped the sweat from his face and carefully looked around. After a few more minutes, he took their reins and led them through the brush following the trail that brought him here. The tracks were there, but since they were going single file through the thick brush, it was difficult to tell how many there were.

He was moving very slow and searching the area all around as far as he could see. He had been shot at once, and it was only by chance that it missed. He wasn't taking any more chances than necessary.

He continued following the trail, knowing he was a sitting duck if they were waiting for him again.

He reloaded his pistol and dropped it in the holster and removed his rifle from its scabbard, because the rifle held fifteen rounds, while his pistol only held six.

The hair was standing up on the back of his neck and he felt like a naked man walking down Main Street at high noon.

He continued slowly while scanning the brush as best he could. Being on high alert constantly was taking a heavy toll on his energy. He had no other choice. If he stopped to rest for one minute, he might wake up with his throat cut.

CHAPTER FOUR

Through the rest of the morning and into the afternoon, he followed the trail. He wasn't so good a tracker that he could tell how old the tracks were, but reasoning told him they couldn't be more than six hours old. That could put them as much as twenty-five miles ahead of him unless they stopped somewhere. So far, they haven't done that for more than a few minutes at a time. He was worried sick over how Carter was handling that. He was only nine years old and had never had to face anything like this. Clay was hoping and praying he was not causing them any trouble. If he were, they would probably knock him in the head and leave him lying where he fell.

Late in the afternoon, as the sun began to slide down the horizon, Clay knew he had to stop. His feet and legs were sore and hurting from all the unaccustomed walking. He began looking for someplace off this trail to take his break, but everything was so thick with vines and briars. Every branch on every bush was loaded with thorns. There were a few trails, but they were low to the ground, probably made by wild hogs and deer. They were pretty thick around here from the tracks he was seeing.

Finally, just before sundown, he saw another trail branching off to the south. He didn't want to get too far off the track of the Indians and his son, but he needed to get off this trail.

The Indian's tracks continued straight ahead, but he took the branch trail and intended to follow it a short piece to see where it led. It didn't take long to find out. In less than a quarter-mile, he heard noises coming from ahead. He stopped to listen but couldn't make out what it was. What he was hearing sounded like children laughing. He crept forward a little farther, then tied his horses and went ahead on foot. When he went around a bend in the trail, he stopped short and stared. He could hardly believe his eyes. There before him was a cabin with children playing in the yard and chickens pecking the ground. Out back was a small shed with a pen made from sticks with several goats and a few donkeys. The house sat in an opening of several acres. There was a garden with what looked like green vegetables, melons, squash, and other plants that he couldn't recognize from here. The house was made of adobe and was large compared to other adobes he had seen.

He watched for a few minutes until one of the children saw him watching them. She let out a little screech and ran toward the house with the others following. Shortly after she reached the house, a man came to the door with a shotgun in his hands. He looked to be in his mid-thirties, about five-eight, weighing maybe one hundred and fifty pounds. He stood watching Clay for a minute until Clay raised his hand above his head in the sign of friendship, and walked slowly toward the house. He stopped about twenty feet away and pointed to the we'll at the side of the house, and asked, "Do you mind if I water my horses and fill my canteens from your we'll?"

The man just stared, and the children stood big-eyed and looked like they had never seen a white man before. Clay motioned toward the we'll and made the motion of drinking and repeated his question. This time in Spanish, "¿Te importa si regar mis caballos y llenar mis cantinas de tu pozo?"

The man smiled and motioned to the we'll. "¿Te importa si regar mis caballos y llenar mis cantinas de tu pozo?"

"Gracious, Senior." Clay returned to get his horses and led them to the trough beside the we'll. They needed no urging to bury their noses in the water and drink their fill. Clay dropped the bucket into the we'll and heard it strike water. He waited a minute or so until the gurgle from the bottom of the we'll told him the bucket was full. He pulled the rope, hand over hand until the bucket reached the top full to the brim. He dunked his head in and drank until he thought he would pop. The water was cool and sweet, just like back on the farm in Tennessee. He sat the bucket on the edge of the trough and pulled his horses away and tied them to a bush a few feet away. Taking his scarf from around his neck, he dipped it into the bucket and wiped it all over his face and head. That was about the best feeling he had had in a long time. He poured the water into the trough and dropped the bucket into the we'll for a refill.

When he had his fill, he turned to see the man with the shotgun standing a safe distance away watching him. Clay smiled and thanked him again for the water.

Then, to his surprise, the man asked him in broken English, "You look very tired, Senior, you must have traveled far?"

Clay smiled again to cover his surprise and said, "Yes, I have been tracking some Indians who took my son. I have been on their trail for three or four days. I seem to have lost track of the days. Have you seen any Indians come by here in the last day or so?"

"No, I have seen no one. They don't usually come this far off the trail which goes farther that way," as he pointed back the way Clay had come from.

"You have a nice place here. You must have been here a while."

"Yes, my family has been here for four generations. Some of my family lives on the other side of the river, and some farther down that way." He pointed east and west, an indication he had family all up and down both sides of the border.

"How far is it to the border?" Clay asked.

He pointed to the south, "Just over there, not far."

That gave Clay a sick feeling knowing the Indians could cross over into Mexico any time they wanted.

He thanked the man for the water and turned to mount his horse when the man said, "Senior, you would be welcome to share our meal with us. Mama will have it ready in a few minutes. It looks like you could use a good meal."

Clay hesitated a moment. He was anxious to get on the trail again, but he didn't want to offend the man by refusing his hospitality. He looked down the trail and then back at the man. His horses could use the rest as much as he could. He thanked the man again and led the horses back to the bush and tied them.

The sun had already gone out of sight, and the air was getting a little cooler. He followed the man to the house with the children staring wide-eyed from a short distance away.

When they reached the house, the man introduced himself as Jesus Santana. Mrs. Santana was standing just inside the door dressed in a plain, clean cotton dress. She looked like she had worked hard her entire life. She probably wasn't over thirty years old, but she could easily pass for forty. She was a little on the plump side, but it looked good on her. Less weight and she would probably look skinny.

She had a meal ready and on the table when they walked into the house. The table and chairs would seat eight with plates at each setting.

He smiled and introduced himself to Mrs. Santana. She smiled and pointed to a chair at the end of the table and said, "Please be seated, Mr. Wade. We are happy you can join us."

Clay was surprised that they both spoke such good English. The children had said nothing since he arrived. There were four of them, two girls and two boys who looked to range in age from about six to twelve years. The oldest was a girl who was helping her mother put the meal on the table. The other three were sitting quietly with their hands in their laps, waiting to start eating. A large bowl was placed in the middle of the table with steam rising from it and putting off an aroma that was causing Clay to have a hard time controlling himself. He was so hungry he wanted to dive in and devour the entire thing. He had eaten nothing but jerky and coffee since leaving home, and his stomach was growling so loud it was embarrassing.

Finally, when everyone was seated, Mr. Santana said, "Mr. Wade, we hope you have much luck in getting your son back."

Mrs. Santana asked Clay to pass his bowl to her, and she filled it to the brim. Then she filled each of the children's bowls. The stew was served with milk, which he assumed was goat milk, and he was pretty sure that was goat meat in the stew, but whatever it was, it was the best meal he had had since he left home, and he made the best of it. Mrs. Santana kept refilling his bowl until he couldn't hold anymore. He finally held up his hands and said, "No more." He rubbed his stomach, and the children laughed.

There was not much conversation during the meal. The children were we'll behaved and knew their table manners. When they finished eating, they quietly left the table and went back to their games outside.

Mrs. Santana asked, "How old is your son, Mr. Wade?"

"He is nine years old. We have never had any trouble with Indians since we have lived there, almost ten years now. We were not expecting any trouble, and then when he didn't come when called to supper, I went looking for him and found the tracks. I've been on their trail for about four days now, I think. Just when I think I've caught up to them, they slip away again."

Mr. Santana said, "We'll, from here on, the tracking is going to get harder. As you already know, the brush is so thick it's hard to find your way through. The Indians know where the trails and water holes are. If you can stick to their trail through all that, you will eventually catch up. But then what do you do?"

"I'll have to figure that out when I get there. All I know is, I have to get my son back. He's been through so much in his short life. I was gone for five years, from the time he was two until he was seven, so we've only been together for the last two years."

Mrs. Santana asked, "You don't have to answer this if you don't want to, Mr. Wade, but why were you gone for five years?"

"My wife, his mother, was killed in a freak accident. We had just lost our baby daughter the winter before and hadn't recovered from that, and then she was killed. I just lost it. I couldn't stay there with all the memories. So I saddled my horse and rode off in the middle of the night. I roamed all over until I met my current wife. She was being held by a gang of bank robbers up in Wyoming. I was acting as the deputy sheriff at the time, and I managed to trail them to the ranch where they were hiding. When I left there with the robbers, she went with me. I convinced her to come to Texas with me. We were married, and now we have a daughter, and I was reunited with my son after five years. Now he has been stolen from me.

"Mr. Wade," Mr. Santana said, "I have to tell you this, it may help you, and it may make you worry more, but you should know. There is a story going around about an Apache renegade who has been making quite a reputation for himself. I have not seen him, but the word is he is a big black man, very strong, and he is cruel. He likes to hurt people. He goes by the name of Black Wolf. He is supposed to be a black man that was taken as a kid and raised by the Indians. He is a grown man now and is bigger than anyone around, and uses that to his advantage. The word is if someone crosses him, he will beat them to death with his bare hands, and he gets his pleasure out of it. All the Indians are afraid of him. He leads a pack of renegades who go around raiding local ranches, stealing horses and killing the men, and taking the young women and girls. Sometimes he takes young children and brings them back to wherever their main camp is at that time. If this is who has your son, you must be very careful not to fall into his hands. He is very mean and cruel."

"Thank you, Mr. Santana, for telling me that. It doesn't change what I have to do. But I will try to be more careful."

"What do you plan to do now? Why don't you spend the night here and get an early start in the morning?"

"Every minute I am not on their trail, I am falling that much farther behind. Thank you for the nice meal. You have a lovely family. I'll not burden you with my problems any longer." With that, he stood, thanked Mrs. Santana again for the wonderful meal, picked up his hat from the floor beside his chair, and headed for the door.

He led his horses to the water trough and let them drink their fill again. He mounted, waived to the little family, and rode back to the trail he had been following for the last several days. The fresh water and the brief rest were a big help to him and his horses. He continued following the tracks until it got too dark to see, but still, he continued. There didn't appear to be any place where they could leave the trail, so he decided to go as long as his horses could go, or until something happened to make him stop.

Long after dark, as he trudged along, trying to stay awake in the saddle, he was aroused when his horse came to a stop. He slapped his hand to his revolver and tried to see why they had stopped, but everything was total darkness. The trees and brush were too thick for light from the pale moon and stars to penetrate to the ground. He sat listening, trying to determine why his horses were standing with their head up, ears pointed forward, nostrils flared like they smelled and heard something that they wanted no part of.

Clay removed the thong from the pistol and pulled the rifle from its scabbard and dismounted.

CHAPTER FIVE

He heard nothing but trusted his horses to have much better hearing than he did. He dropped the reins to the ground, knowing the horses would stand long enough for him to check out what they were hearing. He eased forward until he saw the glow of a fire a short distance ahead. About the time he was able to see the fire, he heard voices. At first, he didn't understand any of it. But then he recognized it as Spanish, and he was able to pick up a word here and there. He crept closer to hear and see what was going on. Clay listened for a few more minutes and then moved closer. When he was within fifty feet of the men, he crouched down behind a bush to listen. The fire lit up the entire camp. There appeared to be four Indians and three or four other men, not Indians, in the group. A wagon was sitting to one side with four mules tied to the side of it, and three horses tied to trees nearby. One of the men doing most of the gesturing and talking was a huge black man. He must have stood we'll over six and a half feet tall and weigh over two hundred fifty pounds of long, lean muscles. That had to be Black Wolf that Mr. Santana told him about. He was strutting around the fire, waving his arms, and making a speech, and he had everyones attention.

Clay couldn't make out everything he was saying, but it sounded like he was trying to make a deal for something he had to sell. Suddenly he stepped to the side into the shadows and jerked a small boy to his feet and held him at arm's length for the white men to see. Clay almost jumped to his feet when he recognized Carter. Before Clay realized what he was doing, he had his rifle aimed at the big black man. He was shaking so bad he probably couldn't hit anything if he pulled the trigger. He held the sights on the black man, and if he made any threat to harm Carter, he would be a dead man.

Carter had tears running down his face, but he wasn't making a sound. Clay was proud of him. Despite the situation, Carter was being very brave for a nine-year-old.

Clay knew if he fired a shot, he might kill Black Wolf, but there was no way he could get Carter away from them without one or both of them getting killed.

He forced himself to calm down and relax and bide his time. His chance would come sooner or later.

Black Wolf stomped around the camp, dragging Carter with him until he finally threw him to the ground and approached one of the white men holding his hand out like he was asking for money. Finally, the white man nodded his head, and Black Wolf smiled and reached out to shake hands. They shook, and Black Wolf said something to one of the other Indians who took Carter and tossed him onto the back of one of the horses.

A few minutes later, they were mounted, and Black Wolf pointed to the sky, and Clay understood him to say, "When the sun is high tomorrow."

The four Indians and Carter galloped away, heading west with one of the Indians leading Carter's horse. Clay watched until the four white men settled down and looked like they were going to spend the night here, so Clay eased back to his horses and moved back up the trail a mile or so and settled down to await the coming day. From what he had seen and overheard, it appeared Carter was going to be sold to the white men who Clay assumed were human traffickers. Carter would probably be taken into Mexico and sold as a slave. Just the thought of it had Clay's blood boiling.

He made a cold camp and spent a restless night getting very little sleep. He tossed and turned most of the night, and when he finally gave up on sleeping, he was more tired than when he went to bed. He made a breakfast of jerky and water while waiting for enough light to make his way back to their camp.

When the sky was just beginning to show some light in the east, Clay saddled his horse, and leading the second one, returned to the spot where he observed the meeting last night. He left his horses hidden in the brush and approached on foot. When Clay saw the glow of the fire, he eased in behind a thick bush and stretched out on the thick carpet of leaves. He had a good view of their camp when they began to stir. All of them looked exactly like what they were, the scum of the earth. They all were dirty with long hair and beards, and their clothes were filthy. He imagined he could smell them even from this distance.

He watched as the camp came alive. The smell of coffee had him wanting to walk in and get a cup for himself. "Enjoy it while you can." He whispered, "If I have my way, it will be your last cup."

Then he noticed there were only two men there. Last night there were four. There were still four mules tied to the wagon and two horses tied to trees nearby.

He was a little confused about the missing men but suspected it had something to do with the meeting at high noon today. But one horse was missing. Then the hair on the back of his neck stood up and he got that feeling of being watched. Just as he began turning his head to check his surroundings the voice came from behind him, "One move and you're dead." The voice came from the right rear of where Clay was lying and sounded like it was only a few feet away. His heart skipped a beat, and he knew he was in deep trouble. The man could not have slipped up on him without being heard, so he had to have been there when Clay arrived, but he was concentrating on the men around the fire and didn't see the one hiding nearby.

"Ease your hand back and toss the pistol over here." All kinds of options went through his head in a flash. Could he take this man and avoid being captured? But, if he took a bullet, that would leave Carter at the mercy of these men. He decided in an instant his best option was to play this hand and see what happened. Maybe another opportunity would present itself with less risk.

Clay slowly eased his hand back and slid the handgun out of the holster and tossed it to the side. All the while, his mind was working to find a way out of this bind. "Now, throw the rifle over here." Clay pitched the rifle aside. "Now, stand up and walk to the fire."

The men at the fire heard the commotion and were standing with guns drawn when Clay and his captor walked into the camp.

"What you got there, Joe?"

"I don't know yet. I caught him spying on the camp and thought I'd invite him in to join us."

Joe gave Clay a big shove with the butt of his rifle, "Get over there and sit down."

Clay sat with his back to the wheel of the wagon.

"That was right thoughtful of you. What do you plan to do with him?"

"I suspect this is the one Black Wolf spotted following him. Let's wait and see what he wants to do with him. That might be fun to watch."

Clay's mind was racing to think of a way to get out of here before Black Wolf arrived. He knew he would be in even more trouble then. It was bad enough with these three, but when the four Indians came, and one of them being Black Wolf, his problems would more than double.

While they were talking, Joe shoved Clay over onto his stomach, took a strip of rawhide and tied his hands behind his back, and tied his feet together.

Then the questions started. "What are you doing spying on us, fellow?"

"I wasn't spying," Clay said, "I was riding through and heard voices. I just wanted to see what was taking place before I rode into your camp."

"That's a likely story. Where were you headed when you just happened to stumble onto our camp?"

"I have a ranch up near Cuero. I heard there was a fellow down this way with cattle to sell. I was on my way to check it out."

"And just what is this fellow's name that has the cattle to sell? Maybe we can take them off his hands and save him the trouble of finding a buyer?" They all laughed at Joe's joke.

"It was Santiago, or Santa Anna, or something like that," Clay answered.

"Santa Anna?" Joe said in surprise. "You dumb gringo, Santa Anna was killed forty years ago, don't you know nothin'? What's your name, Hombre?"

"My name is Clay Wade. What's yours?"

Joe laughed and looked toward the other men. "The gringo wants to know my name." They all thought that was funny.

Joe got serious and looked into Clay's eyes with a mean, threatening frown on his face, "You are very funny, Gringo. We'll see how funny you are when Black Wolf gets hold of you."

"Hey, Joe," One of the other men called out.

"Yeah, what is it, Alfredo?"

"I've been thinking if we turn him over to Black Wolf all he's gonna do is torture him to death. He won't be worth anything then. I think we ought to hide him in the wagon and take him and the kid down to Manuel Ortega. He'll pay us top dollar for 'em. What we get for this hombre will just be a bonus. The Niño is costing us a few horses that Jake is out stealing right now."

Joe pushed his hat back and scratched his head. "You know, that makes a lot of sense."

Clay listened to all their talk and liked their idea. He wasn't looking forward to being the guest of honor at Black Wolf's party. That would also get him back together with his son. Maybe then they could work their way out of this mess.

Joe called to his two buddies, "Y'all give me a hand with getting him in the wagon. I don't want to have to untie him and then retie him. Let's just pick him up and throw him in there."

Alfredo and the other man, Fernando, strolled over and grabbed a leg, Joe took Clay's shoulders, and they carried and dragged him to the back of the wagon. They dropped him to the ground while Joe lowered the tailgate of the wagon. When it was open, Clay was lifted and shoved into the wagon. Joe pulled an old dirty blanket over him to conceal him from prying eyes. The tailgate of the wagon was slammed closed and a pin was inserted to keep it in place.

The blanket was so dirty he could barely breathe. Dust got in his eyes and nose and with his hands tied behind his back, he couldn't wipe his eyes or nose. He sneezed several times in quick succession and tried to maneuver so he could rub his face on something. That wasn't working we'll at all. Finally, by pushing with his feet and elbows he was able to move around until he bumped into something. He kept pushing his head against the object until the blanket covering his face fell to one side and he saw what looked like a bag of food. He was able to rub his face on it and relieve some of the discomforts. Plus it got the dirt and dust from the blanket away from his face and he could breathe much better. The men were talking a few feet away by the fire, but he couldn't make out much of what they were saying.

Things got quiet for a while and Clay guessed it must be close to midday when he heard horses come into the camp. He remembered some of the conversations he overheard earlier about someone out stealing horses to pay for Carter. If he understood Black Wolf yesterday he would be back at the high sun to exchange Carter for the stolen horses.

Someone said, "It's about time you got back. Black Wolf is due here any time now, and he was not going to be happy if these horses were not here. What took you so long?"

The man spoke with a heavy Mexican accent, "The camp where the horses were supposed to be was moved farther up the river. It took me much time to find them. Then there was the guard who wouldn't go to sleep. I waited and waited, finally, he dozed off and I took the horses from right under his nose. Then I took his pistol and hid it under his saddle. Then I put the pretty little flower in his holster where the gun was." He laughed and slapped his thigh, "He es goin' to be so mad when he wakes up."

Clay couldn't tell who was saying what, but it sounded like Fernando said, "That was taking a big risk. What if he woke up and caught you? What would you have done then?"

"I would have conked him on the head with his own pistol."

There was more laughing and joking for a while then things got quiet again.

Clay even dozed off for a while and got a few minutes sleep until he was awakened by the sound of more horses rushing into camp. He tried to sit up so he could hear better, but his space was too cramped to allow that. He lay quietly and listened as the new group charged in. Then he heard the gruff voice of Black Wolf. "You got horses?"

Then what sounded like Joe's voice said, "Yeah, we got your horses. That's them right over there."

Clay was straining his ears to hear anything about Carter when Black Wolf said, "Good, here boy. You make good trade." Then there was the sound of something hitting the ground and horses turning and leaving. As the sound diminished Clay heard one of the men say, "Put him in the wagon and let's get out of here before he changes his mind and comes back. Fernando, you follow them a piece and make sure they keep going. We don't want any surprises if he decides to pull something sneaky. It wouldn't be the first time he doubled crossed someone he was doing business with. Alfredo, you follow us with Wades horses."

Clay listened as they gathered their things and hooked the team to the wagon. Then the tailgate dropped and Carter was thrown into the wagon, and the tailgate closed.

"Boy, you stay in there and keep your mouth shut. If you try to run away I'll catch you and cut your tongue out. You got that Kid?"

"Yes Sir." Carter whimpered.

The dark interior of the wagon kept Carter from seeing the contents of the wagon for a few seconds until his eyes adjusted to the dim light. When his eyes fell on Clay they opened wide and he started to say something until Clay shook his head and hissed for him to be quiet. Carter was shocked, happy, and excited all at the same time. Tears flowed from his eyes leaving streaks where they mixed with the dirt. Carter fell across his dad and hugged him. That's when he realized Clay's hands and feet were tied. Clay shook his head and whispered, "Wait until we get away from here. Our time will come. Do you still have your pocket knife?"

Carter felt his pants pocket and whispered, "Yes." Black Wolf never gave a thought to a nine-year-old having a knife, so they never searched his pockets.

The man they called Joe climbed to the seat of the wagon and slapped the reins on the horse's backs. The wagon lunged forward and made a sharp turn then straightened out on the rough trail across the country. Clay and Carter bounced around until they were able to find a position where they could brace their feet against the sides of the wagon to help hold them in place.

The wagon was completely covered except for the small opening in front behind the driver, and another small opening in the back. Through the opening in the back, Clay could see two riders following the wagon and leading his two horses. One was driving the wagon and one was off following Black Wolf.

After they had been moving for thirty minutes or so Clay whispered to Carter, "Take your knife and cut me loose."

Carter quickly removed the knife from his pocket, opened the blade, and slashed the rawhide thongs holding Clay's wrist behind his back. Clay rubbed his wrist to get the circulation flowing again. He then took the knife and cut his feet free. With the driver concentrating on his driving Clay was able to move around to get a look outside the wagon. He sat down beside Carter and whispered to him, "We will have to be patient until we get a chance to make a break. Now is not a good time.

Maybe after they stop for the night we can come up with a plan. Why don't you get some sleep? I'll wake you if anything changes."

"I'll try, but I don't think I can sleep."

Carter lay down with his head resting on his arm and was asleep in a few minutes.

CHAPTER SIX

Clay tried to relax, but with the wagon bouncing across the rough terrain that was not easy to do. The afternoon sun beat down on the canvas top making the temperature inside the wagon almost unbearable. Dust filtered in through the cracks in the floor and sides making it hard to breathe. He had pulled and worked at the rawhide strings binding his wrist so much they were raw and causing him quite a bit of pain, but there was nothing he could do about that. He was just glad to have his hands and feet free. If, and when, the opportunity came he would be able to take advantage of it.

After several hours of suffering through the heat and dust, it began to get darker as the sun sank lower in the west. The temperature in the wagon dropped a little and became more tolerable. Carter continued to sleep beside Clay. He kept snuggling closer to Clay's side and jerked and whimpered from time to time. Clay put his arm around him and held him close and whispered to him that everything was going to be ok.

When it was almost too dark to see inside the wagon, they came to a stop. They heard orders being given to unhook the team and set up camp. The one called Joe stuck his head in the back of the wagon. When he was satisfied that everything was as it should be he grunted and walked away. A few minutes later, Clay heard someone breaking sticks, and a few more minutes the flicker of fire was casting shadows on the walls of the wagon. Satisfied that they would be busy for a while, Clay eased to the back of the wagon and peeked through the opening. Everyone was busy doing something to get the camp set up for the night. He didn't see his horses, so he quietly eased to the opening in the front. From there he could see all the horses and mules staked near a stream a few yards away. None of the men seemed to be paying any attention to them.

Clay eased back next to Carter and lay down and acted like he was still tied. It got darker and he couldn't see a thing. Suddenly the canvas covering was pulled open and the one called Joe stuck his head in and said, "Here's a plate, share it with the kid, or not, I don't care." The flap was closed and everything got quiet outside. Clay didn't know how they expected him to eat with his hands tied behind his back, but he wasn't going to call it to their attention. He took the plate and shook Carter to wake him so he could eat. He didn't know when Carter had eaten last, but Clay hadn't eaten since early morning, and his stomach was thinking his throat had been cut.

Carter came awake with a start. His eyes were big and he had a frightened look on his face until he recognized Clay. He lunged at him and threw his arms around his neck and held on with all his strength, making whimpering sounds and shaking like a leaf. After a minute or so he calmed down and Clay whispered and asked him if he was hungry. "I don't know. I'm so scared I can't tell."

"Here, try to eat something." Clay whispered, "We have to keep our strength up because were going to get out of here tonight, and it may be a long night."

"We are?"

"As soon as they all go to sleep, and let's just hope they don't post a watch."

"What do we do if they do?"

"We'll have to handle that the best way we can. In the meantime, eat and rest, were going to need it."

They ate all the food on the plate and set it aside. They watched the men around the fire as they ate and drank from a bottle they were passing around. As the night wore on they got louder and louder. Their speech got slurred and they laughed at the slightest thing. Someone staggered over to the wagon and peeked in. Satisfied with what he saw he mumbled something and walked away. The camp gradually got quiet as one by one they each found their beds and turned in. Clay and Carter watched and listened, waiting for the right time to make their break. An hour after they heard the last sound from the men, Clay eased to the front opening and looked out. His heart sank and he cursed under his breath. They had a guard posted near the horses. He was walking around and smoking to help him stay awake. Clay watched him for a while trying to come up with a plan. Just when he thought the man was going to sit down and hopefully doze off, he went back to the camp and shook one of the other men to relieve him. Clay watched him for a long time, hoping for an opportunity they could take advantage of, but they were very experienced at this and never let their guard down.

Every two hours, like clockwork, the guard changed, and Clay stayed awake all night waiting for his chance which never came. As the sun was rising the next morning, the camp came alive. Some of the men were suffering from hangovers, but they never relaxed their vigilance, so he never had a chance to do anything.

Clay lay down and pretended to be tied up as they had left him. Carter was still sleeping, and Clay didn't disturb him. The team was hooked to the wagon and shortly thereafter they moved out. All day they traveled. The dust filtered in and the heat became almost unbearable again. With the canvas cover closed, except for the two small openings, there was no breeze. The air was stifling hot and thick with dust. Clay removed his bandana and tied it over Carter's face, but he had nothing to cover his own face.

Hour, after hour they traveled until Clay thought they would never stop. There were always men behind and in front of the wagon and their heads never stopped turning from side to side. It appeared that they had probably been ambushed before and were not taking any chances of it happening again.

Night came and they continued. The temperature dropped enough to be almost comfortable in the enclosed wagon. Clay assumed they must be nearing their destination and wanted to get there before they stopped.

Finally, two hours after total darkness, the wagon stopped. There was some murmured talk between the men and one of them rode off into the night. The others sat quietly and waited. Clay could hear them talking amongst themselves, but he couldn't understand what they were saying. The driver turned around and looked in the wagon, but it was too dark for him to make out anything, so he turned back around and said something to the others and they waited some more.

After what Clay assumed must be after midnight the rider came back. There was more excited conversation and they started moving again. About a half-hour later, Clay heard dogs barking, and a few minutes later they came to a stop. He heard new voices and smelled smoke from a campfire. A few minutes later the tailgate dropped and a man said, "Ok, the ride is over, get out of there." Clay was still supposed to be tied up, so he didn't move. Carter was sleeping and he didn't move. "Come on, get out of there!"

Clay asked the man, "How am I supposed to do that being all tied up like this."

The man grunted and said, "Ok, stay there, I don't care." The tailgate was slammed shut and the man walked away grumbling to himself.

While Carter slept Clay tried to make himself comfortable, but he was so tense not knowing what was going to happen next. He eased over to the opening and peeked out. Several fires were smoldering and he could see a few tents and hovels scattered around, but he couldn't make out much else. From what he could see this looked like some kind of permanent camp, or maybe a place for these men to dispose of their contraband? In any case, it looked like their chances of escape were reduced considerably.

CHAPTER SEVEN

Clay dozed off and on the rest of the night until he noticed there was more light in the wagon. He knew it would soon be daylight and he and Carter were still cooped up in the wagon. There had never been a chance to make a break since they arrived at this camp. Things were going to get lively when they came to check on them and discovered Clay was not tied. He figured the longer they were held captive the less their chances of escape. In his right hand he held a heavy club that he found among the junk in the wagon, and the first chance he got he planned to use it and take his chances.

The camp gradually came to life around them. Clay was sitting on the floor of the wagon beside the rear opening waiting for someone to stick his head in. He quietly nudged Carter and whispered for him to wake up and get ready for whatever happened. Carter was groggy for a few seconds until he remembered where he was. His eyes got big and he whimpered until he recognized Clay sitting beside him. He looked around with a frightened look and asked, "What's happening?"

"I'm waiting for someone to come and check on us," Clay whispered, "When they do; we are going to make our break. Get your boots on and be ready. We're going to have to move fast." Carter came alive quickly and was ready to go in a couple of minutes.

They waited and waited until Clay began to think everyone had forgotten about them. About the time that thought flashed through his brain he heard footsteps approaching. Clay motioned for Carter to be quiet and moved as far back into the corner beside the opening as he could. He was standing as tall as he could, but he was bent over at the waist due to the low height of the cover on the wagon. When the cover opened and the head came in and yelled, "OK, everybody out," the club came down on the back of his head. He crumbled and was falling back out of the wagon when Clay grabbed him by his collar and belt and pulled him into the wagon. The first thing he did was grab the man's gun and check outside. No one seemed the wiser as to what was happening in the wagon. Clay quickly stuffed a dirty cloth in the man's mouth and tied it behind his head. Then, using the rawhide string they used to tie his own hands and feet, he tied the man's hands behind his back, and then he bound his feet together and pulled them up behind the man and tied them to his hands. He was not going anywhere until someone turned him loose. Clay quickly checked outside, and still, no one was paying any attention to what was happening at the wagon. Clay removed the man's gun belt and strapped it on and checked the loads in the pistol. Only three unfired rounds remained. "What idiot walks around with his gun half-empty?" Clay quickly removed three cartridges from the belt and shoved them into the empty slots and quietly closed the gun and peeked outside again. He looked around as far as he could see trying to locate the horses. They were not on this side of the camp. He moved to the front of the wagon and peeked out. All the horses, including his two, were in a corral about a hundred feet straight out in front of the wagon. No one was watching them, and from here it looked like a clear open run to the horses. He needed to see what was on the side of the wagon and where all the other people were. He took Carter's folding pocket knife and slit a small hole in the side of the wagon cover, just enough to let him see the rest of the camp on the right side of the wagon. He did not like what he saw. A group of men and women, looked like about six or eight, some were sitting and some standing around a fire. Some of the men were passing a whisky bottle around. He moved to the other side of the wagon and made another small slit in the cover. When he pressed his eye to the hole and looked out, he saw nothing but trees with lots of underbrush. Again he checked to make sure no one was coming, and quickly cut a long slit across and another one down from the top of the cover. He stuck his head out and seeing no one, he crawled through the hole and turned to lift Carter to the ground. "Get in the brush and stay out of sight from the camp and go to the corral and get our horses saddled and wait for me."

From the fire area, he heard a man call, "Hey, Joe, what's taking you so long?"

Clay eased to the back of the wagon and slowly peeked around the corner just in time to see one of the men ready to stick his head in the back of the wagon. Clay lifted the pistol and brought it down on the back of the man's head just as he was bringing it back out of the wagon. Clay grabbed him as he was falling and dragged him behind the wagon and out into the brush. There he stripped him of his gun and gun belt and searched him for anything else that he thought he might have a use for. All he came up with was a couple of dollars in change, some matches, which he put in his pocket, a pocket knife, which he also put in his pocket. He took a quick look toward the corral to see if Carter had made it that far. Someone was in the corral and the horses were moving around like something was disturbing them. He checked the loads in the pistol he had just removed from his latest victim. It held five rounds, so he slipped another one in the empty hole and closed the gun. Taking another quick look around the camp and not seeing anyone, he rushed back out to the backside of the wagon and peeked around the corner. Three men and several women were still sitting and standing around the fire. One woman was standing off to the side not taking part in the conversation. He wondered what that was all about, but at the moment he had other things on his mind.

With a pistol in each hand, he stepped from behind the wagon and was halfway to the group before one of them noticed him and pointed. All of them turned in his direction and the two men started to go for their guns, "NO, I wouldn't do that. You would never get it out of the holster before you died. Now, both of you slowly, with your left hand, unbuckle the gun belts and let them fall to the ground." When they had done that he told them, "Now, step back about ten steps."

He stuck his left-hand pistol in his belt and picked up the gun belts and slung them over his left shoulder.

One of the women yelled, "What have you done with Joe and Al?"

Clay told her, "They'll have a headache when they wake up, but they'll live if you behave and do what I tell you."

The woman was acting hysterically and charged Clay with both hands extended like she would gouge his eyes out. Before she could reach him, the red-haired woman who had been standing off to the side reached out and grabbed the charging woman by the hair and jerked her to the ground. Before Clay could react, both women were hitting, scratching, pulling hair, screaming, and seemed to be doing their best to kill each other. Clay didn't know what brought this on, but it was causing a distraction that he didn't need right now.

When it looked like the red-haired woman was doing the most damage, he reached down and took her by the arm, pulled her off the other woman, and pushed her to the side. "What was that all about?"

"Why did you stop me?" she screamed, "I'm going to gouge her eyes out and pull her hair out!" and then she charged into the other woman again.

Clay stepped between them and said, "Stop it or I'll put a knot on your head. Now get over there with the others and behave."

Clay was keeping a close eye on the rest of the men and women as all this was happening, never knowing when one of them would take a crazy notion to do something stupid.

The red-head was crying and shaking, sobbing, wringing her hands with tears running down her face. She was staring at Clay like she was expecting him to do something, but he didn't know what. The way she was looking at him was making him uneasy. He glanced behind him quickly, thinking maybe someone was coming up behind him, but there was no one there.

"Now, here is what we are going to do. We are all going to take a stroll over to the corral. I am going to saddle my horses and ride out of here. If you are smart you won't interfere. If you are not smart, we'll, you take your chances, but they aren't very good. Now move."

Clay stayed ten feet behind them so they wouldn't have a chance to jump him before he could get a shot off. The woman who was crying was hanging back just in front of Clay. Just as they reached the corral Carter came out leading their two horses. "Bring the horses over here Carter, and then open the gate and run the rest of them out."

The crying woman turned to Clay and said, "Please, take me with you. They've been holding me here for over a week, I want to go home, please, take me with you."

"Are any of you other ladies being held here against your will?"

When no one said anything, Clay told Carter to saddle another horse. The woman ran to the fence and told Carter, "That black one is mine." She crawled through the fence and ran to the horse that came to her as soon as she was through the fence.

She grabbed a bridle off the fence and slipped it on the horse and led him to a saddle and told Carter which one was hers. Carter had the horse ready to go in about two minutes. He opened the gate and the woman rode behind the rest of the horses and drove them out of the corral. Carter ran back and mounted one of the horses. Clay removed all the rifles from the remaining saddles and checked the saddlebags for any other weapons. He gave a rifle to Carter and the lady and mounted his horse and galloped out following the other horses and hurrying them along.

Ten loose horses were running before them, all headed north. Clay, Carter, and the woman fell in behind and kept them running for almost an hour until their horses began to tire. Clay put the heels to his horse and galloped around the herd and brought them to a walk. They kept that pace for another hour when they came to a small water hole in the bottom of a gully. The water didn't look good enough for humans, but the horses didn't seem to mind at all. They gathered around and drank until they had their fill, and then moved into the shade of a small grove of trees nearby. Clay and his companions followed the horses to the shade, dismounted and removed the canteens from their saddles, and took a short drink. Clay shook the canteen and was disappointed to discover there was only a small amount left in it. "Carter, how much water do you have in your canteen?" Carter shook it, and with a disappointed look said, "Not much, maybe a quarter full."

Clay turned to the woman, whose name he didn't know yet, and asked her the same thing. She was still drinking and took a moment to answer. "Mine is almost full."

"Good," Clay said, "We will need to go easy on the water. I have no idea how far it is to the next water. By the way, I guess we should introduce ourselves since we will probably be traveling together for a while. I'm Clay Wade, this is my son Carter."

The woman was still nervous and looked frightened. Clay assumed it was because of what she had recently gone through at the hands of that gang of cut-throats, and she did not know him either. Finally, she said, "I'm Alice Taylor."

"We're glad to meet you, Alice, how did you end up with that bunch?"

"I'm from Victoria; those men grabbed me when my husband and I were on our way home from town. They came out of nowhere so suddenly we didn't have a chance to do anything. They knocked my husband out with a rifle butt, and one of the men grabbed me and threw me across his horse in front of him and rode away with me kicking and screaming until he got tired of hearing me and stuffed a dirty sock in my mouth. He told me to behave myself or he would slit my throat and I believed him. I kept quiet until they dropped me to the ground sometime later, I don't know how long it was, but it seemed like a long time. They then put me on my horse and tied my hand to the horn of the saddle. They led the horse until we came to that camp if that's what you want to call it, about three days later."

"How long were you held there?"

"I don't know, I lost track of time, but it must be two weeks or more. It seems like forever. They weren't very nice to me, but I didn't give them any reason to be either. Every time one of them came near me I flew into him like a wild cat, that's how I got all these bruises."

"We'll, you are out of there now and we'll have you home in a few days if we can stay ahead of them, and any Indians who may be around." When Carter heard the word Indians his head popped up and his eyes got big, "Pa, you think we'll run into more Indians?" Clay heard the fright in his voice and tried to make light of it, "Oh, I doubt it, I haven't seen any signs to indicate there are any in this area, but we'll keep our eyes open and play it safe."

Alice also was looking around nervously at the mention of Indians.

Clay said, "We have a few more hours of daylight, so let's cover some more ground before we stop for the night. Alice, how about you take the lead and I bring up the rear. Just keep heading in that direction and keep your eyes open. Carter, you ride directly behind her and help us keep a lookout while we ride. We don't want to ride up on something unexpectedly."

They plodded along in single file in the heat of the afternoon, stopping every couple of hours to give the horses a sip of water from their hats. It wasn't much, but it helped to keep their spirits up and got them through the worst of the heat. The sun went down and it got cooler.

Clay called for a halt as soon as the sun was behind the horizon. There were a few scattered mesquite and oak bushes around, "Let's stop here and see what we have to eat. Carter, do you feel like gathering up anything you can find that will burn? While you're at it lookout for rattlesnakes. Try to get only dead wood, we don't want to send up smoke signals and let everyone know where we are. How are you doing, Alice?"

"I've been better, but I'll make it."

"Good girl, why don't you sit down there by that tree and try to get some rest. Once it's dark we'll move on a few miles, and then call it a day. How does that sound?"

"That sounds wonderful."

CHAPTER EIGHT

After scrounging through the brush and trees, Carter came up with an armful of small branches that had fallen off the trees. Clay got a fire going just large enough to heat the coffee pot. Alice was sitting with her back to a tree with her head drooping, dead to the world. Clay looked at her for a moment and shook his head. Carter came up to Clay and whispered, "She looks like she is worn completely out."

"Yes," he whispered, "I'm sure she has been through some rough times these last few days. Let her sleep until the food is ready."

While Clay was putting their meager supply of food together, Carter loosened the girths on the saddles and gave each of them a few sips of water while he talked to them and gave each a bit of attention.

The only food they had was a little coffee and jerky that was in his saddlebags left over from before he was captured. He made a small pot of coffee and put some of the jerky in a pot of water and let it simmer over the fire until it was soft enough to eat. When it was ready he asked Carter to wake Alice. He didn't want her to wake up and see a strange man leaning over her, after what she had just been through. Carter gently shook her arm. She came awake and went into her defensive mode with her hands in front of her face, doubled into a fist ready to start swinging. When she realized where she was, she said, "Oh, I'm sorry, Carter, it's just gotten to be a habit. I hope I didn't scare you."

"Oh, no Maam, I just wanted to tell you the food is ready if you feel like eating something."

"I feel like eating a horse, saddle and all."

"We can't let you do that; you would have to walk then."

"Yeah, I never thought of that," she said laughing. She got up from the ground, straightened her clothes the best she could, and ran her fingers through her hair, "I must look a fright. I hope y'all don't think I look like this all the time."

"No, maam, I can tell you're a pretty woman when you get cleaned up."

"Why thank you, Carter, you're a regular gentleman."

"Thank you," Carter said as he blushed and returned to the fire.

Alice came to the fire trying to straighten her hair and clothes, to no avail, "I don't know what that is, but it sure smells good."

"We'll," Clay said as he stirred the jerky in the pot, "it's some of the most delicious jerky to be had anywhere around. In fact, it's the only jerky to be had anywhere around here."

She laughed and said, "I'm sure it is, and I'm going to savor every bite."

They only had two cups, and since Carter didn't drink coffee, he drank water from his canteen. Alice and Clay ate the jerky directly from the pot, picking it out with a knife, and sipping their coffee. It wasn't quite dark when the last of the coffee was poured into their cups and Clay kicked dirt on the fire to extinguish it. Alice helped pack away the few cooking utensils, stood and stretched her back. "I sure dread getting back in that saddle. I'm not used to riding this long at one time. But, I know I have to do it to get home, so I may as we'll stop thinking about it and do it." The cinches were tightened and the three riders climbed into the saddles. Alice groaned and made an ugly face when her bottom hit the saddle. Carter laughed, blushed, and looked away.

An hour later, just as the moon was coming up, they found a small grove of trees and thought this would be as good a place as they were going to find to spend the rest of the night. They unsaddled the horses and staked them on the little bit of grass that was nearby, threw their bedrolls on the ground, and were asleep in a few minutes. The horses were close enough that Clay was expecting them to let him know if anything was moving nearby. Several times during the night he heard them moving around searching for something to eat, but never did they seem alarmed or excited about anything. He dosed in and out of a light sleep and the slightest sound had his eyes popping open. He looked first to the horses and then listened into the night. When he didn't hear anything, and the horses were quiet, he dozed off again. Just as the sky was beginning to get lighter in the east, he was up and saddling the horses. When they were ready to go, he shook Carter and Alice, "Come on sleepy heads, we need to get moving." They both came awake quickly and looked around to get their bearings. They rubbed the sleep out of their eyes, stretched, and slowly crawled from their blankets. Carter was up, had his blankets rolled, and tied in a bundle in a couple of minutes. Alice was having trouble with her hair and clothes, but there wasn't much she could do about it. "Don't look at me. I know I'm a mess."

Clay said, "Hey, don't worry about it. We are anxious to see how pretty you are when you get all cleaned up."

"It can't happen too soon for me."

All through the day, they rode northeast. The dust, heat, and bright sun were torture, but they had no choice but to endure it. They suppressed the urge to mention it, knowing it would only bring it to their attention and make them notice it more. The horses were wet with sweat and were allowed to stop to take a breather when they came to any kind of shade, which was very seldom. The country was very barren, with only a few cacti, scattered sage, and occasionally patches of small cedar trees, too small to be much help. Horny toads, lizards, and an occasional rattlesnake were the only other living things they encountered.

Clay kept a constant eye on their back trail. He had the feeling that someone was back there following them. He learned a long time ago not to ignore it. It had probably saved his life a few times so he wasn't taking any unnecessary chances now. If it was just him, he would lay up just off the trail and see who was following, but he had Carter and Alice to think about, and he couldn't put them in more danger than they were already in. From every rise in the terrain he searched behind them and in front. He didn't want to spend all his time watching behind and ride into more problems because of his negligence.

It was mid-afternoon, the hottest part of the day, and the horses were suffering from the heat and lack of water. They had just reached the top of a small hill and saw a few trees in the distance. Clay pointed them out to Alice, who was still out front, "Let's head for those trees down there. There may be some water. At least we will have some shade. We can wait out the worst of the heat."

Clay stopped his horse and turned to check their back trail one last time before heading for the trees. He was sure missing his binoculars. Someone had laid claim to them while he was a prisoner. He could surely use them now. He watched for several minutes but saw nothing to indicate anyone was back there. But he still had that feeling of being watched or followed. When he reached the trees he was pleasantly surprised to see a small stream, more like a seep, coming from a spring beneath a big cottonwood tree. He dismounted and fell to his knees and began digging in the sand to create a hole large enough to hold water. It took him several minutes to get it scooped out. The water was coming slowly, but it eventually filled the hole, and after the sand settled to the bottom they would have plenty of fresh water to drink and fill their canteens. They stretched out in the shade and relaxed while the water seeped into the hole. After about thirty minutes the hole had enough water in it to dip his canteen in and let it fill. The water was cool and sweet. He took a swig and handed the canteen to Alice who took a swig and passed it to Carter. After each of them had taken a drink he poured the rest of the water into his hat and watered the three horses. It wasn't enough to satisfy them, but it would keep them from suffering too much until the hole was refilled and he could give them more. They laid in the shade, chewed on jerky, and rested and kept an eye on the water as it slowly seeped into the depression he had dug. Each time it got deep enough he refilled his canteen and gave the horses a drink. It took over two hours for everyone to get their fill and fill all their canteens. By then the sun was getting low and things were a little cooler. When another hour had passed, the horses were watered again, and everyone took another long drink. Then the canteens were filled again and they moved out.

From the top of the next rise, Clay stopped and checked their back trail. There it was, just what he had been feeling all day, a small dust cloud. It was hard to tell just how far with the evening shadows making everything indistinct. He watched for another minute or two, turned his horse, and caught up with Alice and Carter. "Let's pick up the pace a little while it's cooler and the horses are rested."

For over an hour they rode at a trot and then slowed to a walk for another hour. The moon came up in a clear sky and gave off light enough for them to see where they were riding, but the horses had put in a long day, and it was time to stop for the night. They dropped the saddles to the ground, staked the horses so they wouldn't stray, unrolled their blankets, and crashed where they fell. They all slept like the dead until the sun was shining in their face. Clay jumped to his feet and quickly looked around, but everything seemed to be calm. The horses were standing where they left them the night before and gave no indication that anything else was around.

Clay shook Carter and Alice, "Hey, are you going to sleep all day? You've already missed breakfast, so all you will get to eat today is water and jerky. Get up, let's go."

Carter looked around, rubbed his eyes, and stretched, "I missed breakfast? What did I miss?"

"I had a delicious serving of cold jerky, topped off with a warm cup of spring water to wash it down. Now, aren't you sorry you overslept?"

"No, not really."

Alice added, "I'm with you, Carter, I've had about all the jerky I can stand. But I guess it is better than starving. Although I can't compare the two since I haven't tried starving, yet."

"We'll, if we don't get a move on you may get your chance."

Carter and Alice crawled out of their blankets and proceeded to get ready for another long day of riding.

Clay was keeping a sharp eye on their back trail. Although they had ridden late into the night they had overslept this morning. That could have caused them to lose the advantage they gained last night. He was nervous and anxious to get moving. He kept urging them to hurry without giving them the impression that danger was right on their heels. He had no proof anyone was there, but the feeling was too strong to ignore.

Clay took the lead and moved out at a slow gallop and held it for the first half-hour before slowing to a trot for an hour and finally back to a walk. By then it was too hot to be pushing the horses that hard.

Carter had dropped back fifty yards or so and Alice rode up beside Clay and quietly asked, "You are worried about someone following us aren't you?"

"Why do you think that?"

"Because I've seen how you are constantly checking behind us. Have you seen anything back there?"

"I didn't want to worry you and Carter, but I have this sixth sense that we are being followed, but I could be wrong."

"But you don't believe that any more than I do, do you?" she asked.

"The odds are not in our favor, so I think it's best to not take that chance, and we still have a long way to go."

Carter trotted up beside them so they changed the subject. "How much longer before we get home, Pa?"

"It'll be a few more days. We need to see Alice gets home safe first, and then we can head on home."

"I appreciate what you're doing. I was about ready to kill myself before you two showed up. That was the most miserable I have ever been in my life." She choked up and started to cry.

Clay pointed off to their left, "That looks like smoke over there. Let's check it out." They rode until they could see over the next rise. Spread out before them was a settlement made up of several buildings with smoke coming from the chimneys of several of them.

Alice said, "Oh good, maybe we can get a good meal and a bath, but maybe not in that order."

Clay was checking every building, alley, and open space as they rode into the only street if it could be called that. It was just a trail through the brush that went between the buildings. There was no sign to indicate that there was a name for this place. It looked like it was settled at the junction of three streams, so they had a good supply of water if nothing else.

They rode slowly through the town looking for an eating place and a bathhouse. At the far end, under a large cottonwood tree stood a small building with a sign hanging over the door that read, "EATS".

From the outside, it didn't look too appetizing, but they were so hungry they couldn't be choosy.

They tied their horses to the hitching post in the shade and pushed their way in through the screen door. Inside was totally different from the outside. The wood floor was spotless, clean tablecloths on the four tables, curtains on the windows, and a delicious smell coming from the kitchen.

Alice took a deep breath, "Oh, I'm in heaven. I don't know what it is but I'll take a double helping."

Carter laughed at her and said, "Me too."

Clay was still standing at the door looking up and down the street. A few people were stirring, but nothing looked suspicious, so he came in and took a chair facing the door.

"We'll, this is a pleasant surprise. I hope the food is as good as this place looks on the inside and not the outside." He whispered.

As soon as they were seated, a pleasant-faced, slightly plump lady approached the table, "Welcome, I'm Melba Jones, this is my place, what would you folks like to eat today? We have beef stew, served with cornbread, butter, mashed potatoes with cream gravy, black-eyed peas, and apple pie for dessert."

All three of them were smiling when Clay said, "Say no more and just bring it on. Could we start with coffee for the lady and me? Do you have something for the lad?"

"How about a sarsaparilla? It ain't cold, but it is refreshing."

Carter was beaming from ear to ear, "Thank you, Maam."

When Alice took the first sip of her coffee, she said, "That's the best coffee I ever tasted."

"What? Are you saying you didn't like my coffee on the trail?"

"Your coffee was the best around. I couldn't find any better."

"There must be a compliment in there somewhere. I'll have to think about that."

The food was placed on the table in bowls and dishes so they could serve themselves. They ate until they were hurting and then ate some more.

Carter was dozing in his chair, but he was still poking food in his mouth.

When the waitress came back to refill their coffee cups, Clay asked her if there was a place where they could get a room for the night.

"No, we don't have anything like that. I'm sorry."

"Is there a good place to set up camp for the night?" He asked.

"There's a pretty spot down by the river just on the north side of town. If you follow the trail out back it will take you right to it."

"We think there may be someone following us who aren't very friendly, so if anyone comes in asking if you have seen us, you don't know anything, can you do that?"

"I ain't laid eyes on anyone that even resembles you."

"Thank you."

"By the way," Mable said, "I start serving breakfast at six, so anytime you want to drop in it will be ready."

They lingered over their coffee and apple pie longer than necessary, and when they were ready to leave Clay had to carry Carter out to his horse. He roused up enough to stay in the saddle until they reached the river and their camp. Clay lifted him from the saddle and laid him on the ground until he had the bedroll unrolled. He placed Carter on it and covered him with a blanket.

Alice walked down to the river bank and was looking at the water when Clay walked up behind her.

"That water sure looks inviting."

"We'll, what are you waiting for, dive in. I'll get a fire started and unpack what we have to unpack, so take your time."

Clay returned to the camp and got a small fire going. He kept it small to not attract any undue attention. He heard the water splashing as Alice enjoyed her time in the water. When she finally returned to the fire, she looked like a different person. She was still wearing the same clothes, but her face was clean, and her hair was wet and hanging down her back.

Clay told her, "If you would like to wash your clothes, you can wrap a blanket around you while your clothes dry by the fire. They should be dry by morning."

"That sounds like a good idea." She took a blanket from her bedroll and went back to the river. There was more splashing as she washed her clothes and hung them on bushes at the edge of the water. She returned to the fire wrapped in a blanket from her chin to her feet and shivering from the cold water.

Clay had laid out their bedrolls around the fire, but not too close, since it usually didn't get that cold around here until just before daybreak.

For some reason, Clay felt safer than he had the last several days. Maybe it was because they were close to the settlement. He couldn't bring himself to call it a town, but he slept we'll most of the night. As was his habit, he awoke off and on to listen to the night sounds and glance at the horses. Everything was quiet, so he drifted back to sleep.

Just as the sky was getting light in the east he was wide awake and stirring the fire to life to put the coffee pot on when he remembered breakfast would be served at six. He shook Carter and Alice and got them up with the promise of a good breakfast and more good coffee and sarsaparilla.

They packed all their supplies and saddled the horses and left them tied to the bushes behind the café. He saw no logic in putting them out front to advertise their presence. Clay went to the front corner of the building where he could see up and down the street. Nothing looked out of place so he returned to the back and they went in through the back door. Mable looked up in surprise when the door opened, but then her face lit up in a big smile. "We'll, there you are. Did you all have a good night's sleep?"

Alice answered, "Yes we did. I slept like a log, but the bath was the best thing of all."

Again Clay took a seat facing the door where he could see everything that moved along the street. They were just finishing their second cup of coffee and sopping up the gravy from their breakfast when he suddenly stiffened and pushed his chair back. Alice noticed his reaction and asked, "What's wrong?"

"We have company, you two get to the horses and wait for me down by the river, hurry now."

Clay dropped a handful of change on the table and rushed out the back door after them. He took up a position about twenty feet from the door behind a tree where he had a good view if they should follow him. He heard the two men as they came in the front door and took seats at a table.

As soon as Mable got a good look at them she knew they were trouble. Both were dirty with long scraggly hair and beards, and she could smell them from where she was standing behind the counter. One was tall and gangly, the other was shorter and heavier, but it would be hard to decide which one was the dirtiest.

When Mable went to serve them one of them asked if a man, woman, and boy had come through here the last day or so.

She politely told them she had not seen anyone fitting that description. Then the tall one pointed to the table with the dirty dishes still on it, "Who was eating there just before we came in?"

"Oh, that was a couple of cowhands that come by every so often, they are gone now, I just ain't had time to clean the table, and will you be having coffee for starters?"

They were still looking at the table when the second man said, "Looks to me like three people were eating at that table. Why did you lie to us, woman?"

Mable turned without a word and went behind the counter and brought a double-barreled sawed-off shotgun up and laid it on top of the counter pointed directly at the two men and said, "You two can leave now, or you can stay and we'll bury you on boot hill. What's it gonna be?" as she pulled both hammers back and waited for their decision. Both men held up their hands and said, "Hold on lady, we didn't mean nothin'."

"You heard me, out!"

"Ok, ok, were going, be easy on that trigger, you could hurt somebody with that thing."

"If I lay eyes on you again that's exactly what I intend to do, now get!"

They just about fell over each other getting out the door. A moment later she heard their horses galloping away to the south. She went to the door and looked out to be sure they were gone before she put the shotgun away.

From his position outside the back door, Clay heard most of what transpired inside. He went to the front corner of the building to check the street. When he was sure they were gone he went inside and thanked Mable for what she did. "You know you didn't have to do that, you could have gotten yourself hurt. And you better be careful, they may decide to come back to get even."

"I hope they do, my trigger finger ain't had no exercise in a while."

Clay thanked her again and made sure he left enough money to pay for their breakfast and left by the back door.

CHAPTER NINE

He was almost to the river where Carter and Alice were waiting for him when he heard horses coming through the brush and trees. He had a bad feeling about who that would be. He hurried to get to Carter and Alice before the men did. He was almost there when he heard a mans voice say, "I told you, Coley, that woman lied to us, look what we got here. Black Wolf is sure gonna be pleased with us. He might even let us have the woman for a day or two."

"Yeah, she, I mean that, would sure be nice. It's been a while."

Clay was coming up behind the two men as they sat on their horses looking at their latest catch.

Both men stepped down from their horses and were approaching Carter and Alice, who were standing by their horses watching them approach. Carter was inching closer and closer to Alice for protection, and she was looking for someplace to go. She recognized them from the camp where she was held captive for so long. They had not changed clothes since she saw them last. They were still just as dirty and smelly as she remembered.

Just before they got within reach, Carter yelled, "Run Alice!" He darted to the left while Alice made a break to the right. Before either man could make a move, Clay spoke up from behind them, "Don't move a muscle, I have a gun pointed right at your back." They froze and slowly looked at each other, and then slowly looked back over their shoulders to see who was behind them. When they recognized Clay as the one who had stolen the boy and the woman from them, they were trembling with fury. The first thoughts that went through their heads were that he was going to kill them, and the second was to go for their guns and kill him. At least they would have a chance. If they waited they would have no chance at all.

"Now, very slowly, unbuckle those gun belts and let 'em fall to the ground. I won't tell you twice."

They hesitated a couple of heartbeats and then glanced at each other. Clay knew what they were going to do. He could read it in every movement of their body, so when they made their move he was ready. Each man threw himself to the side in opposite directions and drew their weapons as they were falling. It was like shooting apples in a barrel. They never got off a shot. Both lay moaning and clutching their chest with blood oozing out between their fingers.

Clay kicked their guns out of their reach and said, "That was a stupid thing to do. Did you think you could pull that off? If you did, you're even dumber than you look."

Clay heard a commotion behind him and whirled around and dropped to one knee with his gun ready to fire, "Don't shoot, it's me, Mable!" She was there with her shotgun and looked like she was ready to tackle a grizzly bear. She was breathing hard and her hair was standing up in all directions, "I heard shooting …and I just knew …these two had doubled back… and found you."

Clay lowered his revolver and dropped it into his holster and stood up. "You were right, thanks for coming, but thankfully you were too late, the party is over."

"We'll, we won't be bothered with those two anymore. That's a blessing."

Within a few minutes, both men had stopped moving. Clay went through their pockets but only found a few coins and makings for cigarettes.

"Do you have a shovel I can borrow so I can bury them?"

"No, you've done enough. I'll get a couple of men from town to do that. You all need to get going in case they have friends around who may come looking for them."

"Thanks, Mable, we really appreciate your help. They do have friends, and they have been riding with a renegade apache called Black Wolf. I have seen him in action and he is nobody to fool with. If you see him, you'll know him. Don't take any chances. Shoot him on sight. He is bad news, and he is riding with three other Indians."

"Thanks," Mable said, "I'll spread the word. You people be careful now, you hear."

Mable went back to her café and Clay, Carter and Alice headed north following the river hoping to avoid Black Wolf and his party. After several miles, they turned back to the northeast and picked up the pace. The horses were rested and everyone was anxious to get home.

Late that afternoon they came to a lake that Alice recognized as being not too far from home. They made their way around the lake and camped on the east side just before dark. They found a thickly wooded area and made their way into it until they came to a small clearing. A large tree had blown down and limbs were scattered everywhere, providing plenty of deadwood for a fire. The huge trunks provided a good place to lean back and rest their backs. A fire was built a few feet out from the tree. They had intended to buy supplies before they left town, but circumstances prevented that, so they were still surviving on jerky and coffee. With any luck, they would have Alice home sometime tomorrow. She was showing signs of anxiety both ways. Worried about how her husband was going to react, and wanting to get home. She was taking some comfort from the fact that Clay and Carter would be with her when she had to face Carl for the first time. She didn't want to put them in any danger, but she couldn't help being afraid for her own safety. She had seen Carl act strangely too many times to put any trust into how he would accept, or not accept, the fact that she had been kidnapped and held captive for over two weeks. And, there was still the threat from Black Wolf. He was back there somewhere, and they didn't think he had given up yet.

Carter was rolled in his blankets and asleep within minutes after finishing his meager supper. Alice and Clay were sitting by the fire finishing off the last of their coffee when Clay asked her, "What are you nervous about? You'll be home tomorrow."

"I just don't know how my husband is going to take it when I get back."

"What do you mean?" Clay asked, "He knows you were kidnapped, surely he'll be happy to see you."

"I don't know. He has some strange ideas about women who have been kidnapped and held captive. He thinks they are soiled, and that's not acceptable to him."

"Alice," Clay said, "He knows and you know, it wasn't your fault. Look at what happened to him, he couldn't prevent that either. So how can he blame you for what happened to you?"

"I don't know, but he'll find a way, believe me."

"Pardon me for saying it, but it doesn't sound like he's easy to live with."

"Most of the time he's not. When he first came to work for us he seemed like a good man, but recently he has gone off the deep end. Once he makes up his mind about something there is no changing it.

We had a horse once that kept getting through the fence onto the neighbor's property. Carl would bring him back, but the next day he would be over there again. Every time he would beat the horse. I was so mad at him I could have killed him. I told him if he would repair the fence the horse couldn't get out, but he didn't want to hear that, he blamed the horse. After about the fourth time that happened, he shot the horse. The fence is still not fixed."

Clay mulled that over a few minutes before saying, "He sure sounds like a hard man. How old is he?"

"He's fifty-one, twenty-three years older than me."

Clay was surprised at that answer, and asked, "How is it that you married a man that much older than you?"

She hesitated a moment, took a deep breath, and told the story.

"He was working as a hired hand on the ranch. He was a big, slim, good-looking man in a rugged sort of way. I sort of had a crush on him. I was just a girl, fourteen years old at the time. My father died that year and my mom and I had nowhere else to go, no living relatives that we know of. Carl, that's my husband, said he would stay on and help us run the ranch as long as we wanted to stay. Since we had nowhere to go, we thought it would work out. But right away Carl started making advances toward Mom. She didn't encourage him, but she didn't want to make him mad and make him leave either, since he was the only help we had."

"Things went along fine for a while, but then Carl started getting more aggressive, and Mom finally told him to leave her alone or leave. He seemed to accept that and everything was fine for a few weeks. Then, one day they were out working cattle, and Mom was thrown from her horse and hit her head. She was dead when Carl found her. Or so he said. He brought her back to the house and we buried her there."

"By then I was sixteen years old, too young to own property, and too inexperienced to run a ranch. Carl was so sweet and nice through the whole thing. Again he promised to stay on and help me run the ranch. But a few weeks later he informed me he had been appointed by the county judge to be my legal guardian until I turned twenty-one. I didn't know what that meant, but a few days later he moved all his things into the house and took over Mom and Dad's room, which was just across the hall from my room."

"I didn't see a problem with any of that. I didn't like living in that big house alone, and I didn't know anything about running the ranch. I could cook and clean and do any of the other chores around the place, but it takes a man to manage a ranch."

"At first he treated me like a daughter, but he soon started flirting with me and making suggestions. I laughed it off as good fun and played along with him. Then things changed. He started getting serious."

"Then one night as we were eating supper, he told me there were men in town who were talking about taking the ranch away from me because I was a minor and a female, and neither could own property in Texas. He said they were working on the judge to give them title to the ranch. He scared me so bad that when he proposed marriage as a way to keep it I jumped at the idea. I thought things would remain as they were, with him in his room and me in my room, but he had other ideas. As soon as we got home from town with the marriage license he took me into his room and forced himself on me. He said it was his right as my husband. From that day on I have hated him with every bone in my body, but there was nothing I could do without losing the ranch, the only home I have ever had."

"As time went on, it got worse. He started drinking and coming home drunk and forcing himself on me in his drunken state. I've thought of killing him many times, but as bad as he needs killing, I can't bring myself to do it."

Clay was shaking his head in disbelief, "Alice, I would like to help you get out of this mess with Carl if I can, but I don't know what I can do without killing him, and I'm not a killer.

Oh, I've killed plenty of men, too many, in fact, but it was in the war, or to save my life or my family. Have you attempted to talk to the judge or the sheriff about your situation?"

"No, when were in town, he never lets me out of his sight. It's almost like he's afraid I'm going to talk to someone. We go into the store and get what we went after and come home. Sometimes he goes alone and comes home drunk, but he never leaves me alone when we go there together, and I never get a chance to go alone."

"Where is the county seat for your county?" Clay asked.

"We are in Victoria County, the county seat is Victoria."

"Ok, why don't we stop in Victoria on the way and talk to the judge or a lawyer. See if there is anything you can do short of killing him."

"That sounds so.....gruesome. I can't believe we are even talking about killing my husband." She shivered.

Clay hesitated a moment, "I don't think we are actually talking about killing him, that was just a figure of speech. We'll figure out something. You wait and see."

"I hope you're right. I'm so afraid of what he will do when he sees us together. He'll think the worst and take it out on me."

"No, he won't, I'll guarantee that." Clay said.

"How can you guarantee that? You don't know what he's like or what he'll do, and you won't be around long. What's going to happen after you leave?"

"You're right about that, but let's see what happens. It can't be that bad." Clay said, hopefully.

"I hope you're right."

Carter was dead to the world. He had stayed with them, step for step from the beginning, but he finally ran out of steam and needed his rest. Alice was nodding beside the fire when Clay touched her on the shoulder and told her he was going to move away from the fire so he could hear anything moving. "I won't be too far, so if you need me for anything just call out, I'll hear you."

She nodded her head, but he didn't know if she understood what he had said or not.

There was a patch of underbrush about thirty feet from the fire, so he pushed his way into the middle of it and settled down with his back to a small tree. He dozed a few minutes and roused up and looked at the horses sleeping on their feet nearby. That went on until two or three in the morning when he finally fell into a deep sleep. The next thing he knew Alice was handing him a cup of coffee and the sun was just peeking over the horizon. He jumped up and asked, "Why did you let me sleep so late? Those men could have snuck in on us and cut our throat and we would never have known it."

"I've been awake for several hours. You were sleeping so soundly I didn't have the heart to awaken you. Drink your coffee, the horses are saddled and ready to go, we are just waiting on you."

"You sure know how to make a guy feel unnecessary."

She laughed as he climbed to his feet and wiped the dew off his rifle. Out of habit he checked to make sure there was a round in the barrel, set the safety, checked his handgun and wiped it clean, and dropped it back into the holster.

Carter was humped over the fire sipping on a cup of hot coffee. His face said he didn't like the taste, but it was the only thing they had to drink, except water.

Before they started on the way home, Clay rode back up the trail a piece until he could see down their back trail. What he saw sent chills up and down his spine. Not more than two hundred yards away, and coming straight at him, were six riders, and the one out front was a big black Indian. He was riding a big black and white paint horse with eagle feathers braided into his mane to match the ones in Black Wolf's hair. He was naked from the waist up and carried a rifle resting on his left thigh pointed at the sky. The rest of the group was made of the three Indians who regularly rode with Black Wolf and two white men. Clay only got a glimpse, but he thought they were two of the men from the camp where he escaped with Carter and Alice.

He wheeled his horse and raced back to their camp. When he got close enough to see Alice and Carter, he started motioning for them to get mounted, quickly. He didn't know if they understood his signals or not, but they knew something was wrong from the way he was riding. Everything was already packed, so all they had to do was mount up. When Clay raced into camp all he said was, "Let's go!"

They didn't ask any questions, but put the spurs to their horses and did their best to keep up with Clay. He raced through the grove of trees knowing they were leaving a trail anyone could follow, but they had no choice. If Black Wolf and his gang caught them they would stand very little chance of getting out of this alive.

They raced straight away from their usual trail at a ninety-degree angle hoping their trail wouldn't be discovered until they had time to come up with a plan. He stayed behind the trees and brush as much as possible. He didn't know if he was doing a very good job of it or not, since he didn't have time to be too careful.

They rode hard, doing their best to remain out of sight. After a half-hour of riding as hard as the horses could manage, he pulled them to a halt just after they crossed a small rise. He motioned for them to stop while he rode back just far enough to see over the hill and check their back trail. With just the top of his head and eyes looking over the hill, he couldn't believe what he wasn't seeing. There was no one back there. He watched for a couple of minutes, still not believing they had gotten away when they were so close.

Alice asked, "We'll, what do you see?"

"Nothing."

"Nothing, you mean we got away from them?"

"We'll, for now anyway. But I don't believe Black Wolf is that easy to fool. Let's keep moving. I don't like the looks of this."

Clay rode to the top of the next rise and took a long look in all directions. "We need to keep moving northeast. Sooner or later we are going to get to something that you recognize, I hope."

All day they rode watching in every direction expecting Black Wolf and his gang to pounce on them at any moment. They stopped and listened often, and at every hilltop, they checked their surroundings, but it appeared they had managed to escape without being seen.

Late that evening, just before sundown, she pointed out the entrance to her place. There was a gate in a fence that ran out of sight in both directions. The gate was dragging on the ground and needed to be re-hung. The fence was sagging in places and most of the fence posts were rotted and leaning. This confirmed what Alice had told them about how Carl was taking care of things around the place.

When they reached the gate, Clay dismounted and pushed it open and let Alice and Carter ride through and then closed it. The ride to the house was another two hundred yards. Alice was nervous and anxious at the same time.

"You will stay with me until we know how he's going to act, won't you?"

"Yes, we will. Nothing is going to happen to you, just relax and be glad you are home."

CHAPTER TEN

They rode around the house to the barn and corrals in the back. When they dismounted in front of the barn they heard a door slam behind them and turned to see Carl standing on the porch holding a rifle. He did not attempt to approach them or ask about Alice. He just stood looking at them. Clay could see the hatred in his eyes, and his expression didn't give him any confidence that this was going to end we'll. He looked to be over six feet tall with a few extra pounds around his middle. He had not shaved in a week or more and his dirty shirttail was hanging out over his soiled and wrinkled pants in several places.

Alice heard the door slam and turned toward the house and saw Carl standing there. She dropped the reins and jumped off her horse and ran to him and threw her arms around his neck. "I'm so glad to be home. It was awful; I didn't have a chance to get away until Mr. Wade and Carter came along. What happened to you, I saw them hit you and you fell. That was the last thing I saw before they hauled me away. What happened?"

He made no effort to hug her or ask about what happened to her, or where she has been, nothing that a loving husband would be expected to do when his wife has been kidnapped and gone for over two weeks. He just stood there, stiff as a board, and kept his eyes on Clay.

Alice realized he was not acting friendly and pulled away in fear and looked back toward Clay.

Carl pushed her to the side and said to Clay, "I guess you had a good time with my wife while you had her to yourself?"

Clay was taken aback by the way he was acting, but after what Alice had told him, he wasn't too surprised. He had already removed the thong holding his pistol in place, so when he turned to face Carl he was ready for whatever was going to happen.

He walked to within about six feet of Carl and stopped. He figured at that distance if Carl started to use his rifle he was close enough that he could reach him before he could get off a shot.

He looked Carl in the eye and said, "Yeah, we had a good time. First, we were held captive by a crazed Indian, my son and I, and then we were sold to a bunch of thieves and murderers who planned to sell us in Mexico. Before they got around to doing that we were taken to one of their camps where they were holding your wife and several other women. Carter and I managed to escape and your wife asked us to bring her along. So, for the last several days we have been hiding and dodging renegade Indians and that gang of hoodlums. Yeah, it's been a real picnic, you should have been there, I'm sure you would have enjoyed yourself."

Carl was giving Clay a look that would scare most men down to their boots. Then he said, "You got a real smart mouth, don't you? I have a good mind to teach you a lesson about fooling around with another mans wife." He stepped toward Clay, then came the slap of a bullet striking flesh, his eyes blinked and his hand went to his chest. He looked down and saw blood trickling between his fingers. The sound of the gunshot came a moment later. Carl grabbed his chest, dropped his rifle, staggered back to the wall of the house, and slumped to the floor.

Alice screamed and fell to her knees beside him. Clay dropped to one knee as he pulled his revolver and spun toward the sound of the shot. Coming at them at a full gallop were the six renegades they had been avoiding for the last four days. Black Wolf was in the lead riding his big black and white horse, followed by the other five, all screaming and yelling their war cries. Clay yelled "Carter, get in the barn! Alice, grab that rifle!"

He opened fire as soon as Black Wolf was in range of his pistol. He was taking deliberate aim making sure his bullets were going where he wanted them to go. He knew he had to take Black Wolf out even if he didn't get any of the others. He saw his first shot strike him high in the left shoulder making him slump to the left which gave him a better target for his second and third shots. Black Wolf tumbled off his horse at Clay's feet. The other five were almost to him when he heard a rifle firing as fast as Alice could pull the trigger and lever another round in the chamber. Clay made a mad dash toward his horse to retrieve his rifle from the saddle scabbard. He fired the last three shots in his revolver as he dashed the fifty feet to his horse.

His horse was tied to the corral fence and skittish from all the gunfire, but Clay was able to grab his rifle from the boot as he ran by and made a dive for the barn door. He hit on his shoulder and rolled inside behind the wall, and looked to see where Carter was and saw him crouched behind a feed barrel.

Clay peeked around the door facing to see what was happening outside. Two men were laying in the yard moaning and rolling around with blood soaking the ground under them. One was wrestling with Alice on the porch of the house and the other two were rushing the barn door. They were only ten feet away when Clay stepped out and opened fire with his rifle. He caught both men by surprise. They saw him run into the barn, but they didn't see him grab his rifle as he ran by his horse. They thought his revolver was empty and he would be an easy victim. Clay fired, levered, and fired four shots into them within two seconds. That only left the one fighting with Alice. Clay tried to get a shot at him, but Alice was in the way, or too close to take a chance, so he made a mad dash across the yard just in time to keep Alice from getting a knife in the chest. The Indian had her pushed up against the wall and had his arm drawn back with the knife ready to plunge into her when Clay hit him in the back of the head with his rifle. He crumpled to the floor and didn't move again. Clay took the knife from his hand and stuck it behind his belt.

"Alice, are you ok?"

She slumped to the floor leaning back against the wall and didn't answer for almost a minute. Clay was getting worried until she said, "I think so."

Clay took a quick look around the yard to see if there was any more danger. When he took a count of the bodies lying about he was relieved to see there were six of them and none of them were moving. He could hardly believe they had pulled off a win against six of them, and one of them being Black Wolf. When that word got out a lot of people were going to be mighty relieved.

Then they remembered Carl. He was still lying where he fell when the bullet hit him. Alice and Clay went to him and found he was breathing and had a pulse. Alice opened his shirt to check the extent of his wound and found a bullet hole high in his right chest. There was a lot of blood and he appeared to be in shock. Remembering what he learned from his army days, he elevated Carl's feet and covered him with a blanket while Alice got bandages and heated water.

Clay rolled him over so he could see if the bullet had come out the back, or if it was still in there. When Alice came out with the water and bandages, he told her, "The bullet is still in him. We need to get him to a doctor. That bullet needs to come out or he could die from infection if the bullet doesn't kill him."

Alice thought for a moment, "Ok, there's a wagon behind the barn and a team of horses around here somewhere. They are probably in that pasture over there." As she pointed to where she thought they would be.

"Ok, I'll round them up while you do what you can to get him patched up."

He ran to the barn and found Carter still hiding behind the feed barrel, "Carter, are you alright?" When Carter said he was fine, Clay asked him, "How about you go up to the house and help Alice with Carl. He's been shot. I'm going to get the team and hook them to the wagon so we can take him to a doctor. He's hurt pretty bad."

Carter was pale and his face was streaked with tears but seemed to be recovering now. He took a deep breath and said, "OK", and slowly walked to the house. He was looking at all the bodies scattered about the yard when he saw Black Wolf laying at the edge of the porch. He slowly walked over and looked down at him for a few seconds, and then he drew back his foot and kicked him in the face as hard as he could. He started turning away, but then turned back and spit in Black Wolf's face, kicked him again, and said, "Go to hell."

Clay was concerned about Carter with everything that he had been through the last two weeks, so he watched him as he left the barn to cross the yard. He wished he could protect him from the grizzly sight he was seeing. Bloody bodies were lying around the yard and there was no way to protect him from seeing them. He watched as Carter approached Black Wolf's body, wondering what he was thinking. When he saw Carter kick and spit on him he said to himself, "That's my boy. He's going to be ok."

Carter asked Alice what he could do to help. "If you could help me lift him so I can get this bandage around him to help stop the bleeding, that would be a big help." They got Carl bandaged as best they could and made him as comfortable as possible where he was.

It was thirty minutes or so later that Clay returned with the horses. It only took him a few minutes to get the harness on them and hook them to the wagon. Alice brought a mattress and blankets from the house to put in the back of the wagon to make a bed as comfortable as they could, knowing the ride to Victoria was not going to be easy on Carl.

Clay and Alice picked Carl up as gently as they could and laid him in the wagon. While they were doing it Carl was thrashing about and muttering all kinds of unintelligible things. He was covered with a blanket, although it wasn't cool enough for a blanket, they were afraid he would develop a fever before they got him to the doctor.

Alice quickly grabbed a few things for snacks knowing they were all going to be hungry before they reached Victoria. Because they would need to take it slow and easy the trip was going to take at least four hours, and maybe more.

Alice was driving the wagon with Carter and Clay following on their horses. As they were going out the gate Clay noticed the horses were acting a little strange, but he couldn't figure out why. He took a moment to check their surroundings, but the only thing he saw out of the norm was a black cloud forming to the south and the air had a clean fresh smell to it like there was rain coming their way. He closed the gate and took another moment to look around. He was still nervous from the run-in with Black Wolf and his gang, but he didn't think that was what was spooking the horses. He mounted his horse and caught up with the wagon. He kept looking to his right as they rode and saw the cloud was getting larger by the minute. He was about to say something about it to Alice and Carter when a flash of lightning lit up the sky and thunder rumbled in the distance.

He checked to see if he and Carter had raincoats on their saddles and saw that they did. He rode up beside the wagon pointed out the clouds to Alice and asked her, "Is there someplace up ahead where we can hold up if this gets too bad?"

She took a minute or so to think about the route they would be taking before she answered, "A couple of miles ahead there's an old abandoned barn off to the left. I've only seen it from a distance, so I don't know how weatherproof it is."

The wind picked up and the tree limbs began whipping about. "Better get your slicker on Carter, looks like we are going to get soaked. Alice, do we have anything to cover Carl with?"

She thought for a second, "There's a tarpaulin under him, I didn't prepare for anything like this."

She stopped the wagon and together they pulled the tarp from under Carl and covered him with it.

Clay suggested, "How about if Carter and I ride on ahead and check out the barn? We will meet you there."

Clay removed his raincoat and handed it to Alice, "You'll need this more than I will. We'll try to make it to the barn before the rain hits."

"Ok, I'll get there as soon as I can." She tapped the horses on the back with the reins to speed them up some, knowing it was going to be rough on Carl, but figured it couldn't be any worse than getting soaked with cold rainwater.

They put the spurs to their horses and raced ahead until they saw the old barn. It didn't look like it would stand up to much wind, but it was the best chance they had.

The fence and gate leading to it was not an obstacle since it ceased to serve any purpose long ago. They rode through it and up to the barn with its sagging doors and roof just as the rain hit them. Clay stepped down and pushed the door open enough to see inside. The rain started slowly at first, and then the wind picked up and the rain came down in sheets, slicing across the ground and hitting them before they could get inside. Clay led his horse through the door and Carter rode in and dismounted. Even with the slicker on, he got wet from the knees down, and Clay was soaked from head to toe. Poor Alice was sitting up there on that wagon seat with only the raincoat for protection and Carl was lying in back with only a tarp over him.

When his eyes adjusted to the dim interior, he saw scraps of lumber and abandoned furniture lying about. "Let's get a fire going, Carter. They're going to be wet and cold when they get here."

They gathered the scraps of wood, and anything they could find to burn, and got a fire going toward the back of the barn, but far enough from the walls to prevent the whole structure from burning to the ground. They left enough room in the front part of the barn for the wagon and team to get in. Stalls along one side provided ample space for their horses and the two pulling the wagon.

The wood was dry and only took a few moments to have a nice roaring fire going. Carter was watching through a crack in the door and saw Alice coming with the wagon and had the big double doors open when she arrived. She drove directly inside and looked around. The fire looked so inviting she climbed down from the wagon seat, shaking like a leaf in a storm, ran to it and held out her hands, and turned around letting the heat soak into her body. "Oh, that feels so good, but we have to get Carl out of the wagon. He must be frozen solid."

Carl was still unconscious and they considered that a blessing since he wasn't feeling the rain and cold. The three of them, working together, managed to get Carl out of the wagon and stretched out near the fire. All their blankets and clothes were wet, and all they could do was stand as close to the fire and let them dry at their own pace. They kept Carl covered and he came through pretty we'll except where the wind had blown the tarp off one side and let his blanket get wet. The blanket was hung close to the fire to dry along with all their clothes that they could afford to remove, considering the mixed company.

Outside the storm had really picked up. The old barn shook and creaked and had leaks in the roof and cracks in the walls, but it was better than being out there. The door flew open and crashed back against the outside wall making a tremendous bang like a shot. They all jumped, and Clay's pistol appeared in his hand as if by magic. When he realized what the noise was he looked down at his gun and was stunned for a moment, wondering how that got here. Alice saw the quick draw and looked at him in awe. "Wow, you are fast."

Embarrassed, he put the gun away and added more wood to the fire. The door was still open, but the rain was coming down so hard, he didn't think it was worth going out in it to get it closed. The rain was blowing in but it wasn't reaching as far back in the barn as where they were.

The little bit of food they brought along wasn't going to last as long as the storm, but they got the coffee going and sat around on the discarded furniture items and sipped the coffee, and ate the food.

The clothes and blankets hanging by the fire gradually began to dry and they were finally able to feel the heat soaking into their bodies. Unfortunately, Carl was not doing as we'll. He couldn't get close enough to the fire to get dry, but he was not feeling anything. They kept checking his pulse and his chest was rising and falling, so they knew he was still alive. As the blankets got warm, whether they were dry or not, they removed the wet ones covering him and replaced them with the warm dryer ones.

The day passed with the storm raging outside, and night set in wet and cold. Carter fell asleep beside the fire, and since there was nothing they could do to make him more comfortable, except replace his wet covering with something dryer, they let him sleep. Alice and Clay, wrapped in whatever they could find, sat on opposite sides of the fire, keeping an eye on Carl. From time to time he groaned and mumbled, but they couldn't understand what he was saying.

The storm shook the barn and rain came through the walls and roof, but it was dry enough where they were. Lightning lit up the night and thunder crashed, the barn shook, and they expected it to come crashing down on top of them.

The horses had nothing to eat, but there was no shortage of water, and Clay was able to catch rainwater in an old bucket and give them plenty to drink. Whoever built this barn planned ahead and put it on the highest ground around so there was no rising water coming inside, except through the open door and the holes in the roof and walls.

Toward morning, it was hard to tell what time it was since everything was pitch black outside, the wind picked up and they were sure the barn was going to blow away. The walls were leaning to the downwind side, and shingles were blowing off the roof letting more water pour in. They quickly moved the fire to a dryer spot just before it was drowned out by water pouring in from above. Twice more they had to move the fire to keep it going. Finally, to keep Carl and themselves from getting soaked over and over, they lined the bed of the wagon with their raincoats and the piece of tarpaulin that was in the wagon, and all of them crawled under the wagon to keep dry. The fire was just off to the side which gave off enough heat to keep them from getting too cold.

Carter was so tuckered out he slept through most of the night, only rousing up when they had to move him to a dryer place. Once they were all under the wagon and wrapped in their sleeping bags and blankets, they were fairly comfortable. They felt safer under the wagon in case the barn did come crashing down they would have some protection.

Carl was still mumbling under his breath, but they were not paying too much attention to what he was saying until he blurted out, "I'll kill that little bitch just like I did her mama. It'll all be mine."

Alice looked at Clay in shock, and asked, "Did you hear what he said? Did he mean he was going to kill me and did he kill my mom?"

"I don't know, Alice. That's what it sounded like, but he is so out of it he doesn't know what he's saying."

They started paying more attention to his mumblings after that, but he said nothing else that they could understand.

The storm continued to rage outside and more rain poured in. The horses were getting restless with no food and the noise of the storm was keeping them on edge. Clay took them two at a time and walked them up and down the hall of the barn to give them some exercise and keep their minds off the storm. That calmed them down for a little while, and then he would have to do it all over again.

Their food was gone, so they could sympathize with the horses, but that's all they could do.

When it was light enough outside to make out objects nearby, they saw trees were blown down and water standing in all the low places. The big double doors to the barn were blocked by a big oak tree lying across it. The thick bushy top closed the door opening completely allowing them no way out. They had no ax or saw to cut the tree out of the way. After surveying the situation in the light of day, Clay decided to wait until the storm slacked off and he could get outside to take a better look around. The wind died down considerably within the last couple of hours and the rain wasn't coming down as hard. The storm had moved off to the north and would continue to get better for them if they could only wait it out a little longer.

After another hour, Clay kicked a couple of boards off the side of the barn and forced his way outside. When he saw the size of the tree blocking the door he knew there was no way they were going to go out that way. The other end of the barn looked like the best bet, so he got busy knocking the wall out. That was a job since the boards had been there for ages and were seasoned as hard as a rock. After almost an hour of struggling, with the help of Carter and Alice, they had a hole large enough to drive the wagon through. The rain was still coming down, but not as hard as it did during the night, and the wind had slacked off to just a stiff breeze. Not knowing how much longer the rain would continue, and since they had no food for themselves or the horses, they decided to take their chances on the road.

They got Carl loaded into the wagon and covered him with the tarp. The rest of them would probably get wet to the skin, but it couldn't be helped.

With the team hitched to the wagon with Alice driving and Carter on the seat beside her, Clay brought up the rear. They pulled out of the barn to a trail that was soggy, muddy, and hard to get the wagon through. The wheels bogged down six to eight inches making it difficult for the horses to pull it through. But once they reached the main road the going was much easier. It was just two wagon tracks, but it had been used for years and was hard enough to support the weight of the wagon,

Three hours later they pulled into Victoria to a sight that wasn't good to look at. Trees were down, houses were without roofs, and some were blown off their foundations. Water was standing two and three feet deep in the streets and houses. Everywhere they looked there was massive destruction. Alice couldn't help wondering what her home looked like after seeing the destruction here. Clay was thinking the same thing about his home and Marilyn and the baby, although Cuero was farther inland and the storm would have blown itself out some before it reached there, he hoped.

Alice knew where the doctor's office was located, so she drove directly there. The house was up on blocks high enough that the water did not reach the floor, but the water was two feet deep all around it. A sign over the door identified the place as Dr. A. William Price. Clay dismounted and tied his horse to the hitch rack and knocked on the door. A man in his fifties, wearing spectacles with a goatee and mustache, opened the door. Before he could say anything, Clay told him they had a badly injured man out here that needed help. "We'll don't just stand there jawing, bring him on in."

"We'll need some help, he's too heavy for me to handle by myself. Do you have a board, a door, or something we can put him on to move him?"

"Yeah, I'll get a stretcher."

He brought the stretcher out and with everyone helping they were able to get Carl inside and on the table in the doctor's office. "What happened to him?"

"He was shot by Black Wolf, the renegade Indian."

"When did this happen?"

"Yesterday, before the storm hit," Clay said

"Where have you been?" Dr. Price asked, "What took you so long to get him here, he could have died from loss of blood or infection."

"We were on our way when the storm hit, we had to hold up in an old barn until it blew itself out."

"We'll, better late than never, now get out of here and let me do my job. Where will you be if I need you?"

"We'll be at the hotel across the street if they have room for us," Clay answered.

"I'm sure they will, ain't nobody out in this storm."

"Nobody except us, I guess. One thing I want to mention, doctor, he's been mumbling about killing someone and said he's gonna kill someone else, so if he says anything you can understand, it would be helpful if you could remember what it was, or even write it down. It might save someone's life. Can you do that?"

"I'll tell my nurse when she comes in to keep her ears open."

"Thanks, Doc. Where's the closest livery stable?"

"Down that way, about two blocks."

Alice and Carter went to get two rooms at the hotel while Clay took the horses and wagon to the livery. When he came back a half-hour later the hotel clerk directed him to room 202. "The lady is across the hall in 203."

He took the stairs up and found Carter already sacked out on the bed. He hadn't even removed his boots, so Clay pulled them off, removed his wet pants and shirt and covered him to his chin with a blanket, and let him sleep. Clay went back downstairs and asked the clerk where he could get something to eat. "There's a cafe four doors down that way. I don't know if they survived the storm or not, but I guess you'll have to go down there to find out."

"How did y'all make out here?"

"We did pretty we'll, considering everything that went on around us. We were protected by the buildings on each side of us so the wind didn't do hardly any damage. The rising water is a concern though. It only came in the front door there, but no damage to speak of, so far."

"Looks like you're one of the lucky ones." Clay said.

"Yeah, looks like it. A lot of people got hit pretty hard."

CHAPTER ELEVEN

Clay left the hotel walking in water two feet deep until he reached the café. It was another one of the buildings high enough to keep the water out. He stepped up on the porch, removed his boots and socks and poured the water out, and twisted the water out of his socks before entering. He was met by the sweet aroma of fresh biscuits and coffee. He couldn't keep from smiling as he took a seat as far from the door as possible.

Although it was the lunch hour there were only four other men in the place. They looked like local merchants, sitting at one table.

They all looked at Clay when he entered and took a seat. The waitress came to take his order and Clay ordered the largest steak they had and a pot of coffee. The coffee came and he took a sip and smacked his lips.

The men waited until he had sampled his coffee and then one of them asked, "You're a stranger around here, Mister, where did you float in from?" They all laughed at his joke.

Clay smiled and said, "You got that right, on both counts. I came from the south and got caught in the storm about three hours out late yesterday."

"Where did you manage to find a place to spend the night, or did you?"

"Yes, you may know the place, it's an old rundown barn down south about ten miles or so, on the right off the road a piece," Clay responded.

"That must be the old Hardin place. Since that boy, John Wesley got in all that trouble and left the county, the place has run down. The house burned down a few years ago, and there wasn't anybody living there then, ain't been anybody around since then."

"Hardin, John Wesley you said." Clay inquired, "That's the gunman that shot and killed Sheriff Helm and his deputy over in DeWitt County a few years back isn't it?"

The man answered, "Yep, that's him. I heard about that. Hardin is some kin to the Taylors in that feud with the Suttons over there. That fight has been going on for years."

Clay took another sip of coffee and said, "We'll, it sure came in handy last night. I wasn't sure it was going to hold up through the night but it was still standing, for the most part, this morning."

The man doing all the talking continued, "You need to be careful down in that country. I heard a woman was kidnapped by Indians a couple of weeks back, and ain't been heard from since."

Clay asked, "What was her name?"

"Taylor, Alice Taylor. I never met her, but I saw her around town on occasion, she was a real looker. That husband of hers kept her under his thumb pretty much when they were in town. Never let her out of his sight, something strange going on there if you ask me."

Clay responded, "Yes, we'll, you are right on both counts. There is, or was something strange going on there. It seems that the husband took advantage of a helpless teenager, pretending to help her, but in reality, he was stealing her ranch from her."

"What are you talking about? How do you know so much about that?"

"I brought Mrs. Taylor in last night. She was being held by a gang of thieves down close to the border intending to sell her in Mexico. And, she wasn't kidnapped by Indians, they were a gang of white men and Mexicans. My son was also kidnapped, and being held by the same people, and then by my own carelessness, I ended up in their hands too. To make a long story short, my son and I escaped, and Mrs. Taylor came along with us. But we were trailed by that gang and an Indian renegade named Black Wolf. They caught up with us just as we arrived at Mrs. Taylor's ranch. We managed to hold them off and kill all of them, but her husband, a man named Carl, I don't think I ever heard his last name, caught a bullet in the chest. He's over at the doctor's office getting patched up. Doc doesn't know if he's gonna make it or not, he's in pretty bad shape."

The talker said, "Might be better for the little lady if he doesn't make it, from what I've seen and heard."

Clay looked at the man for a moment, took another sip of coffee, and then asked, "What have you heard?"

"Oh, just the usual gossip about town, you know, somebody's always spreading rumors."

Clay took another sip of coffee and waited another moment, and then said, "It might be important to the little lady if she knew the gossip. You know the old saying, where there's smoke there's fire. There may be some truth in the gossip." He took another sip.

"All I know is old Carl Krauss has a habit of talking too much when he's had a few too many. He was in the bar one night bragging about how he owned that ranch when someone reminded him that his wife was the rightful owner. He just snickered and said well, she ain't gonna be the owner much longer. When he was asked what he meant by that he clammed up and wouldn't say any more. I guess he realized he had already said too much."

"How we'll do you know this Carl?" Clay asked.

"Not all that we'll. He's pretty much a loner. Comes to town every week or so and drinks, mostly by himself. But he has been seen talking to some strangers on occasion. Don't know what they were talking about, but they acted like they didn't want anyone to hear them. They were sitting back in the corner and had their heads together like they were plotting something. It looked mighty suspicious if you asked me."

Clay asked, "Did you ever see those men around town, before or after that night?"

The four men talked among themselves for a moment, and then shook their heads, "No, can't say as I have."

Clay's breakfast came and he lit in. He didn't realize how hungry he was. He took his time with his meal and coffee, thinking about what he had learned.

When he finished eating, he left money on the table, picked up his hat, nodded to the men, and left the cafe. He trudged through the knee-deep water to the doctor's office to check on Carl. A pretty young lady, who looked to be in her late twenties, standing just over five feet tall with short dark hair, opened the door when he knocked, "Can I help you with something?"

He removed his hat and answered, "I'm Clay Wade, I brought a man in earlier with a gunshot wound, just wanted to check on him, see how he's doing."

"I'm Beverly Davenport, Doctor Price's nurse, come on in."

"No, I'm too wet, I just wanted to check and see how he's doing."

" It's too early to tell. He's not awake yet, but he seems to be in a lot of pain. He thrashes about and mumbles a lot."

"Can you understand what he's mumbling?"

"Not much," she said, "but what I did understand was very disturbing, something about killing someone. Do you know what that was about?"

"Maybe, maybe not, I'm going to talk to the sheriff, he may want to come and talk to you about what you've heard. Will that be ok?"

He got directions to the sheriff's office and walked through the knee-deep water again until he found the sign over the door proclaiming this to be the sheriff's office. He pushed the door open and found about a foot of water covering the floor as far back as he could see, but no one was there. He stepped back outside and looked up and down the street until he saw a saloon sign down about half a block.

The saloon also had a foot of water standing through the entire building, but the patrons didn't seem to mind if they even noticed. Clay stepped up to the bar and ordered a beer. The bartender drew his beer and said, "I haven't seen you in here before."

Clay took a sip of his beer, nodded his head, and said, "Not bad, you're right, first time here. I'm lookin for the sheriff, any idea where he might be?"

"What do you need the sheriff for?"

"We'll," Clay said, "If I wanted to discuss that with you I would have asked for the bartender now, wouldn't I?"

"Yeah, I guess you would. I was just trying to help."

"You can help by telling me where I might find the sheriff."

"Ok," said the bartender, "See that fellow sitting over there that looks like he's about three sheets in the wind?"

Clay turned to look at the man the bartender was pointing out to him, "Yeah, I see him."

"We'll, that ain't the sheriff. That's his deputy, but he might know where Sheriff Thurmond is, but I doubt it."

"Yep, it doesn't look like he will know where much of anything is. You got any other ideas?"

"You could try his house. That would be my next guess."

"And where would I find his house?" Clay asked.

"Go down here to Third Street, turn left; it's the fourth or fifth house on the right. It's the one with the picket fence with the tall gate."

"Thanks and how far is that?"

"Probably farther than you want to walk in all this water."

"That's what I was thinking. But it's just about as far to my horse, so I guess I'll walk it."

Clay left the bar, stopped at the hotel on the way to check on Carter, and again, he had to remove his boots and empty the water before entering the hotel. He found him still sleeping, so he knocked on Alice's door to let her know what he was doing and asked her to check on Carter for him. She said she would, and he began the long walk to the sheriff's house.

By the time he arrived his upper legs were hurting and aching from forcing their way through the knee-deep water. He knocked on the door and waited what seemed like a long time, but he was probably just impatient from being so tired. Finally, the door opened and he was facing a middle-aged man, standing about six feet tall and weighing two hundred or so pounds, about Clay's size, clean-shaven and dressed neatly, with a 45-caliber pistol in his hand. Clay hesitated a moment, removed his hat, and asked with a smile, "I see you were expecting me. You must be the sheriff to welcome me with a shootin' iron in your hand."

"Yes, I'm Sheriff Thurmond, what can I do for you, Mister…?

"I'm Clay Wade, from over Cuero way. I have a delicate situation I need to discuss with you and see if you know anything about it."

The sheriff hesitated a moment, and then asked, "Couldn't it wait until I was at the office?"

"I suppose it could, but I don't live around here, and I don't know when you might be in the office. And, this is pretty urgent. Do you want to talk here or meet me at your office?"

Sheriff Thurmond took one look outside and said, "Let's talk inside." He stepped back and held the door open for Clay. Before he entered the sheriff's house, he struggled to remove his boots again, poured the water out, and struggled to get them on again. He was shown into what was called the sitting room, which was furnished modestly, and was suited for a sheriff's pay. The sheriff called into another part of the house, "Hey, Molly, can you bring us two cups of coffee, please? I assume you drink coffee, Mr. Wade?"

"Yes I do, but just call me Clay."

"Ok, Clay, what's on your mind?"

"Are you familiar with a man named Carl Krauss?"

"Yes, I know the man. He has been a guest in my barred hotel a few times."

"Do you know his wife?"

"Yes, I know her too. What's this about?"

"You may know she was kidnapped, supposedly by Indians, a couple of weeks back."

"Yes, I heard about that. I took a posse out and looked around, but by the time we were notified several days had passed and there was nothing we could do."

"Who notified you of the kidnapping?"

"I believe it was one of the town citizens who dropped by and told me. It seems he heard it in one of the saloons from Mr. Krauss."

"So Mr. Krauss was telling it in the saloon, but he never reported it to you or any law official."

"That's about right."

"Don't you think that was a bit strange?" Clay asked.

"Yes I do, but knowing Krauss, I didn't add too much into it. Where is this going Clay, if I may be so blunt?

"Ok, let me begin at the beginning."

Clay relayed how Carter was kidnapped by Indians and he followed them, was kidnapped himself, which took them to the camp where Alice Taylor, or Krauss, was being held. He told how they escaped and made their way back to Alice's home only to find Carl Krauss was not at all happy to see her return. He relayed how the fight went with Black Wolf and his gang, Krauss getting shot, the storm, riding it out in the old barn, and finally making their way to the doctor here in Victoria.

"Along the way, Mr. Krauss began mumbling things that at first were unintelligible, but then he blurted out how he was going to kill that little bitch just like he did her mama, so he would own the ranch all to himself. I asked the doctor to pay attention to his mumblings, and if he said anything important to let me and you know. I haven't talked to the doctor yet to see if he has heard anything, but Nurse Davenport did hear him mumbling about killing somebody. I wanted to see if you might be able to shed any light on the subject."

Sheriff Thurmond was silent for a long time before he said anything. Finally, after drinking most of his coffee, he cleared his throat and said, "We'll, that kind of ties in with what I suspected for a long time, but I couldn't get any proof. Everything happened out there in nowhere with nobody around, no witnesses, just his word for what happened, and it was weeks before we knew about it. Things started looking suspicious when Krauss and that little girl suddenly got married. I never did know what was behind that, but it sure looked suspicious, especially when he had his name added to the bank account and hers was taken off. But, as I said, I have no proof of any foul play, so there's nothing I can do."

Clay took a sip of coffee as he thought, "Remember back about the time they got married, was there any talk about someone trying to take the place away from her because she was underage and single?"

"No, not as I heard. And I usually hear about things like that from somebody. There are too many busybodies in this town for something like that to be kept quiet."

"How about the judge?", Clay asked, "How tight are you with him? Would he have said something if someone approached him with something like that?"

"I'm pretty sure he would have asked me to look into it, but he never said anything either."

"So you would say there probably never was anyone trying to take the place away from her."

"Yeah, that's what I would say. Where did this come from anyway?"

"According to Alice, Ms. Taylor, Mrs. Krauss, whatever name you want to use, Mr. Krauss told her there were people here in town trying to take the place away from her because she couldn't legally own property because she was too young and single. But, if she was married, then nobody could take it away from her. So, she, being afraid of losing her home, agreed to marry him, assuming it would be on paper only. But Mr. Krauss had other ideas, and before the ink was dry on the marriage license, he was claiming his right as a husband and literally raped her. And then on the way here, after he was shot, he made those remarks about killing her like he did her mom. As you can understand, she is scared to death. And, after seeing the way he reacted when she returned home after being kidnapped and gone for over two weeks, I am not so sure he didn't have something to do with that kidnapping. He sure didn't seem happy to have her back."

"We'll," Sheriff Thurmond said, "As soon as this water goes down enough to let me get around, I'll ask some questions where Krauss hangs out when he's in town. If he said anything, I'll find out about it. In the meantime, where are you staying, in case I need to talk to you?"

"We're at the hotel across from the doctor's office. Oh, we have another problem too, all those bodies out at Ms. Taylor's place. What are we gonna do about them? She's gonna be going home soon and those bodies are gonna be pretty ripe by then. Don't you need to do some investigating, make a report or something?"

"Yeah, you're right. I guess I could send the undertaker to pick up the bodies and bury them, but the county and city would raise holy hell about the cost, so I think the best thing would be to send out a burial crew and just bury them out there. The cost will still be about the same though. How about you ride out there with me tomorrow? You can show me what happened and I'll make my report. We'll have a couple of men bury them and be done with it."

"Ok, what time do you want to leave?" Clay asked.

"Let's let this water go down some, so how about right after breakfast?"

"That sounds good to me."

Clay left the sheriff's house and walked back to the doctor's office. The same pretty nurse told him that Mr. Krauss had regained consciousness and was able to talk to him now.

"I don't want to talk to him, I was checking to see how he was doing."

"It looks like he will make a full recovery if an infection doesn't set in. But so far he's doing as we'll as can be expected."

Clay asked the nurse in a low whisper, "Has he said anything else about killing anyone?"

"There was some mumbling, but we couldn't understand anything he was saying," she whispered.

"We'll, that's too bad; I was hoping he would have said something the sheriff could use."

"What are you talking about, killing someone and something that the sheriff could use? What has this man done?"

"There's nothing to be worried about as long as he is unable to get out of bed."

"But what about when he gets out of bed?"

"Even then I don't think you will be in any danger."

"You don't think?" she asked excitedly.

"We'll, even if what we suspect is true you are not the one in danger."

"We'll, then who is?" she asked.

"Just so you know, but this is not to go any further, ok?"

"Ok," she said.

"On the way here, after he was shot, he said something about killing that woman like I did her mom. The only one we can think about that might be is his wife, Alice Taylor. Her mom supposedly died when she fell from her horse while out riding with Mr. Krauss. Also, Mr. Taylor died under suspicious circumstances while Mr. Krauss was around."

"Oh my!" she exclaimed, "What are we going to do?"

"We'll, for now, we are going to keep our ears open and hope to hear something that may shed more light on the subject. The sheriff is going to come over and talk to Krauss when he can talk."

"I'm not sure I want to be left alone here with that man," she said.

"Before he regains his strength we will take whatever steps necessary to make sure everyone is safe, so don't you worry, Mrs. Davenport."

Clay trudged back through the water to the hotel, removed his boots and socks, walked in his bare feet to Carter's room, and found him and Alice sleeping in Clay's bed. He went across the hall and stripped to the bare skin and crawled in Alice's bed and was asleep in no time. When Alice awakened several hours later and went to her room, she found Clay dead to the world with his clothes hanging on the backs of chairs at the foot of the bed so they could dry. She quietly went about her business and left the room without waking him. When she entered Clay's room she found Carter sitting up in bed rubbing his eyes and looking confused, "Where's my dad?" he asked.

"He's across the hall in my room sleeping. Are you hungry?"

"Yeah, I'm starving."

"Let's go downstairs and see if we can find something to eat, ok?"

"Ok."

CHAPTER TWELVE

When Alice and Carter left the hotel headed for the café down the street, the water had receded enough that the sidewalk was above water. Even the street was visible in places. People were out checking the damage left by the hurricane, sweeping the debris from their porches, and pulling tree limbs away from their houses. The destruction was everywhere. Houses were blown off their foundation and sitting at odd angles. Some had been blown against the house next door. It was going to take a long time to get things back to normal around here.

When they entered the café they found it packed. It seemed like everyone was here talking about the storm and who has the most damage.

There were no vacant tables and they were about to leave when two men stood up and called to them, "Maam, you can have this table we were just leaving."

"Thank you, Sir, we appreciate it."

"You're welcome, Ma'am, fine-looking boy you got there."

"Thank you, Sir."

They took their seats and ordered their food. While they were waiting they listened to the conversations going on around them. Everyone was talking about the storm and how much damage they sustained. She heard her name mentioned and looked to see who was talking about her, but whoever it was looked the other way and pretended they didn't know she was there. She kept listening, but they were whispering and she couldn't hear them. Finally, the food came and they both ate like starving bears. Before they left, they ordered a plate to go for Clay. Carter took it into the room where he was sleeping and shook him to wake him. When he smelled the food he sat up and rubbed his eyes and took a moment or two to get his bearings and realize where he was. "What is this Carter? Did you cook this yourself?"

Carter laughed, "No silly, you know I can't cook, Alice and I got it at the café."

"We'll, I appreciate this, do you want some?"

"No thanks, we ate at the café."

Carter sat with his dad while he ate, and then Clay got dressed in his almost dry clothes and they went across the hall to their own room where Alice was waiting. Clay told her about his visit with the sheriff and what he learned, which didn't amount to much. They agreed that Carter would stay here with Alice tomorrow while Clay and the sheriff went to take care of things at her ranch.

They each slept in their own beds that night and Clay met the sheriff in the café the next morning about sunup. The water was all but gone from the streets and things were getting back to normal around town when they rode out. Two of the town locals rode out with them to help with the burial of the bodies.

When they arrived at the ranch, and the sheriff was getting the details of the fight, they discovered one of the bodies was missing. "He was right here Sheriff, I know I put three bullets in him and he fell right here next to the porch. My son even came over and kicked him in the face, so I know what I'm talking about. So how could he just up and walk away?"

The sheriff was scratching his head and looking around, "We'll, apparently he wasn't as dead as you thought."

"That's sure what it looks like unless dead men can get up and walk away."

Sheriff Thurmond said, "We better check the house and barn just to make sure he's not laying up here somewhere and shoot us in the back. You want to check the barn and I'll check the house?"

Clay drew his revolver and slowly approached the open barn door and peeked around the door frame. At first, he saw nothing out of the ordinary, but when he passed through the door and his eyes adjusted to the dim light he saw something that made his skin crawl. There on the floor in front of him lay a dead cow with one hind quarter cut off. Next to the body were the remains of a fire, apparently used to cook the meat of the cow. A large chunk of meat was missing from the detached hind quarter lying next to the dead fire. Clay forced himself to look away from the grisly sight. After seeing this, he knew without a doubt that Black Wolf was alive and may be hiding in the barn. Chills ran up and down his spine. He took his time searching the interior of the barn by just moving his eyes. When he didn't see anything he slowly moved to the first stall on the right and then proceeded to check the stalls on both sides of the aisle. There was a hayloft above, and when he thought about climbing the ladder and sticking his head up in the dark loft, more chills ran up and down his back and the hair stood up on the back of his neck. He decided to wait until the sheriff joined him, just in case Black Wolf was hiding up there, he would have some backup. He moved back to the door to check on the sheriff while keeping his eyes on the loft. The sheriff came out of the house and holstered his gun which told Clay he had found nothing in the house. He motioned the sheriff to come over, explained what he had found inside. They both pulled their guns again and entered the barn. Clay said he would climb the ladder and the sheriff would keep watch from below. If he saw any movement up there he would shoot first and ask questions later.

Clay slowly climbed the ladder with his revolver in his right hand. When he reached the top he slowly raised his head above the floor of the loft and jerked it back down. When there was no action from above he tried it again, still, nothing happened. This time he removed his hat and placed it on the end of the barrel of his pistol and slowly raised it hoping if Black Wolf was up there he would think there was a head in the hat. Still, nothing happened. Clay replaced his hat and slowly climbed higher until he could see what was up there. Hay was stacked on one side, but the rest of the loft was empty. Upon further inspection, there was no sign that anyone had been there. Clay sighed in relief and climbed back down. Sheriff Thurmond was watching the show and also sighed with relief when Clay reached the floor.

Clay removed his hat and wiped the sweat from his forehead. "That was scary. I don't want to ever have to do that again. Next time you do it."

"Oh no, there ain't gonna be a next time."

"I hope you're right." Clay said.

They holstered their guns and walked outside.

"I wonder where he got off to." Clay wondered. "Obviously he wasn't hurt nearly as bad as I thought. And as long as he's alive he's gonna be looking for revenge, and he knows where this place is and he knows where I live. That is not a comfortable feeling."

"Yeah, I see where you're coming from. I would be concerned too."

The two gravediggers that came with them had been standing back waiting for orders. Sheriff Thurmond walked over to them and gave them instructions to take all the bodies off into the distance and bury them deep. "Make the hole deep enough for that dead cow from the barn and bury her with these varmints. That'll serve 'em right."

While that was going on Clay was looking around the barn to see if he could discover any tracks that might give some clue as to which way Black Wolf went when he left the barn. The ground was soggy from all the rain but there was no standing water except in the lowest places. Clay found moccasin prints leaving the back door of the barn and followed them along the fence until they met up with horse tracks in a grove of trees south of the barn. Clay assumed the horses belonging to Black Wolf and the other renegades had ridden out the hurricane in the trees and were still there when Black Wolf came looking for them. The horse tracks led off to the south which was a relief to Clay since he was pretty sure Black Wolf was headed back to his people to recover from his wounds.

Assuming that he was in no immediate danger, Clay returned to the house and informed the sheriff what he had discovered. They waited around until the burial detail was completed and they all rode back to Victoria. When they arrived they found the city mostly free of water but the streets were still soggy and all the damage was still there. Clay went immediately to the hotel to check on Carter and inform Alice of what they found at her place and that they had cleaned things up, and it was ok for her to go home if she wanted to. "But," Clay added, "Black Wolf is still out there and he knows where you live and that is where he was shot. So I wouldn't be a bit surprised if he showed up looking for revenge. It may be a while, but he will come."

Alice was shaking and wringing her hands, "I don't know. I can't stay here, and I'm afraid to go home. I'll be there by myself. If he came back I wouldn't stand a chance, would I?"

"I'm afraid you're right. Why don't you come home with Carter and me until we can get things straightened out and it's safe for you to go home? You can meet my wife and baby daughter and we'll work things out. I'll talk to Sheriff Thurmond and ask him to keep an eye on Carl and see if he can come up with a solution to get him out of your life."

"That would sure be a blessing if he can do that."

"Ok, that's settled. Let's plan on leaving first thing tomorrow morning."

"Clay, I need to find some clothes. These are so dirty I'm ashamed to be seen in them. Do you think there's a place open where I can buy something?"

"Why don't we ask the hotel manager? He will know where you can find something, or who to ask. If you are ready to go now Carter and I'll walk with you and meet you at the café when you are finished with your shopping."

"I'm embarrassed to be seen like this, but I don't have a choice, do I?"

"It'll be alright; if anyone sees you they will understand. Come on, let's go."

They left the hotel and struggled through the muddy street to the seamstress that the hotel manager directed them to. The shop was open for business, so Carter and Clay left Alice there and went to the café. There were several people enjoying coffee and other refreshments when they entered. One of the men was the same one who talked to Clay the first time he came in during the flood. "We'll stranger, I see you haven't floated away yet. How is the patient doing, is he gonna make it?"

"The doctor seems to think he will, if he doesn't get an infection, or something else doesn't kill him."

"That's good news, I guess, depending on how you look at it."

Everyone went back to what they were talking about before Clay and Carter came in. They ordered their food and Clay sipped his coffee while Carter had sarsaparilla. They had just finished eating when Alice came in looking like a million bucks all decked out in her new clothes. She even had her hair done up in a bun on the back of her neck with a few little curls hanging down around her face. She looked just like a teenager. All the men stared and couldn't take their eyes off her until she was seated at the table with Clay and Carter.

Carter smiled and said, "See, I told you she was a beautiful lady, Pa."

"Yes, you sure did and you were right."

Alice blushed and said, "You guys are embarrassing me, but thank you, Carter."

Alice ordered a light meal and when she was finished, they went back to the hotel. Clay stopped in at the doctor's office to check on Carl and found him sitting up in bed and giving the doctor and nurse all kinds of trouble. He was wanting out of that bed and he wasn't taking no for an answer. The nurse tried explaining to him that he was too weak to be out of bed. He insisted so she told him, "Ok, go ahead and get out of bed. But I'm not going to pick you off the floor when you pass out. You will lay there until you are strong enough to get up on your own."

With that warning, she walked out of the room. Clay was standing in the door and watched Carl throw the sheet back and swing his feet to the floor and stand up. He immediately staggered back and sat on the edge of the bed. After a moment or two, he laid back and pulled the sheet over him. "Give me a few minutes, I'll make it."

Clay left the doctor's office and went to see Sheriff Thurmond and told him Carl was awake and wanting to leave. If he wanted to talk to him now was a good time to do it.

When they walked back into the doctor's office Carl was again sitting on the edge of the bed. Sheriff Thurmond introduced himself to Carl and said he had some questions for him.

"I got nothing to say to you, so get out of here and leave me alone."

"We can do this the easy way or we can do it the hard way, it's up to you. You can talk to me here, or you can talk to me over at my office in a cell. I have all the time in the world, so you can sit there as long as it takes for you to answer my questions. Now, which is it gonna be?"

"All right, what do you want to know?" Carl asked.

The sheriff pulled up a chair and sat down, took out his pipe, and proceeded to stuff the tobacco in and lit up. When it was going to his satisfaction, he leaned back in his chair and looked at Carl, "You made some remarks about killing Alice's Ma and that you intended to kill Alice too. Just how and when did you intend to do that?"

Carl got a frightened look on his face and stammered and sputtered a moment before he could come up with something to say, "I don't know what you're talking about, I ain't never killed nobody."

"That's not what you said last night. You said you were gonna kill that little bitch just like you did her ma and then you would own the ranch all by yourself; those were your exact words. Now you got some explaining to do, Mister, so start talking. How did you kill her ma, and what happened to her pa? That's another question I want an answer to."

Carl was visibly shaken and didn't know what to say. Finally, he blurted out, "You got nothing on me, and I'm not saying another word. Get out of here and leave me alone, can't you see I'm in bad shape and need my rest?"

"You listen to me, Krauss, I'm gonna get to the bottom of this if it takes all year, so don't you even think about going anywhere. As soon as the doctor says you can leave here you are gonna come over and stay with me until I find out what happened out there. Do you understand me, Krauss? And, if anything and I mean anything, happens to that little lady, I'll see you hang."

On his way out Sheriff Thurmond instructed the doctor and nurse to let him know if Krauss tried to leave or caused them any trouble.

Early the next morning as Clay, Alice, and Carter were preparing to leave the cafe, the sheriff stopped them. "I was just informed by Doctor Price that Krauss slipped out during the night while no one was watchin'. I've searched all over town and no one has seen him, but a horse is missing from a stable behind one of the houses a couple of doors down. So you folks better keep a sharp lookout. No telling what he has in mind now that he knows were on to him. My guess is he will go back out to your place first, but after that, there is no telling what he might do. My deputy and I are gonna ride out there and look around, so y'all be careful."

"Thanks for the warning, Sheriff," Clay said, "If you need to get in touch with us you can send a wire to the sheriff's office in Cuero. They will get it to us sooner or later. Ms. Taylor is gonna be staying with us until this mess is cleaned up. With Black Wolf still loose and now Krauss, there is no safe place for her around here."

"I'm sure you're right about that."

From Victoria to Cuero, with good horses, took them five and a half hours. In the mid-afternoon, they stopped at the café on Main Street for a bite to eat since they had not eaten since early morning. Several people they knew saw them riding down the street and waved and wanted to know how things went. They all had heard about Carter being abducted and were curious to know what happened. Clay waved and said, "Everything is fine, we got him back and he's fine."

"We'll, were sure glad to see you back, Carter."

"Thank you, Sir." That was all Carter could say.

They took seats at a table and ordered their food and everyone wanted to know what happened. Clay tried to explain as briefly as possible, but they all wanted the details. Finally, when their food came they were left alone to eat in peace. Another hour and a half took them to the BAR W ranch ten miles to the north of Cuero. When they were in sight of the main house, Carter put the heels to his horse and galloped the rest of the way to the front porch. Just as he was pulling his horse to a stop, Marilyn came storming out the door and grabbed him up in her arms and swung him around, kissing him on the cheek and forehead, with tears streaming down her face, "Oh, thank God, you are safe! Where is your father?" She asked.

Carter turned and pointed back up the road. When Marilyn saw Clay she started running to meet him. Clay jumped off his horse and picked her up in a bear hug and swung her around while kissing her on the lips and squeezing her so tight she couldn't breathe. Finally, when she could talk, she said, "I've been so worried I haven't slept since you've been gone. I'm so glad you are home. Are you both ok?"

"Yes, were fine; by the way, I'd like you to meet Ms. Alice Taylor. She was abducted by the same people that were holding Carter and we managed to steal her away at the same time. She's going to be staying with us for a few days until some other things get straightened out. We'll explain all that later, but now we just need to sit back and relax for a month or two. It's been a trying couple of weeks and even more for Alice."

Marilyn walked over to Alice and shook her hand and said, "I'm glad to meet you, and you are welcome here as long as you want to stay. I can only imagine what you went through."

"Thank you, I'll try not to be a bother."

"Don't worry, you won't be any bother."

Clay and Marilyn walked arm and arm to the house. Alice was invited in and shown to a room across from Carter's room and told to consider herself at home. Carter took it upon himself to show her the rest of the house, and even outside where the outhouse was and the barns. He pointed out all the different horse corrals and promised to show her the horses as soon as she was ready. She was amazed at the size of the operation.

Marilyn brought the baby girl out and put her in Clay's arms and went to the kitchen to put the coffee on, knowing how Clay liked his coffee. She was back in a minute wanting to know all the details, from the minute he left until the minute he arrived back. He gave it all to her in a nutshell and promised to give her the details later. Alice came in and filled in her part of the story and told how Clay and Carter had rescued her from the hands of the gang of thieves, how they were attacked when they got back to her place, and the fight that took place. She skipped lightly over her husband getting shot and being taken to the doctor in Victoria. Marilyn was curious about that and asked Clay about it later when they were alone. He told her that story and how Carl has now escaped and is on the loose. "That, and the fact that Black Wolf is still alive, and knows where she lives, is why she is here. It's not safe for her to be where Carl or Black Wolf can find her. Her life wouldn't be worth a plug nickel."

"Oh, that poor girl, she has been through hell, hasn't she?"

"Yes, and I'm afraid it's not over for her or us. Remember, Black Wolf also knows where Carter and I live, so we have to be on our toes until both of them are out of the picture. I'll go talk to the men and let them know what's going on. We'll set up around-the-clock watches so no one can sneak in on us."

When all the men were in the bunkhouse kitchen later that evening, Clay went out and gave them the complete story, and asked them to set up the watch schedule. All of these men had been with Clay from near the beginning here in Texas. Luke Wilson and Willie Stanton came with him from Tennessee. Lefty Knox, John Williams, Matt, and Gerald Cordis were local men who came to work on the ranch not long after Clay arrived. Wally Wallace, the cook, joined them a couple of years later when Ellen had Carter to take care of and didn't have the time to do the cooking for the entire crew. Ed Carter, Ellen's brother, lived a half-mile away. "We will also need to keep a couple of men around here during the day. So y'all work that out and everyone stay on your toes and keep your eyes and ears open, and your gun handy. At the first sign of anything unusual fire off three quick shots and everyone come running. Got it? Does anyone have any questions?"

When no one said anything Clay returned to the house and told Marilyn and Alice how things would work, since all this was new to them. Clay and Ellen, his first wife, had to put up with this kind of thing when they first came here from Tennessee and had a running battle with the Thompsons and the Smiths. It seemed like they were attacked almost every day by one or the other that first year until the last Thompson was killed and the Smiths decided to leave them alone.

They turned in early that evening and slept late the next morning but awakened refreshed and ready for the new day. Clay checked with the men and learned that nothing happened during the night, and the day started as usual, except for the two men working around the barns and keeping a sharp eye open for strangers. Wally Wallace was also on the alert and was wearing his gun belt and revolver while doing his thing in the kitchen.

On the third day, a rider came from Cuero with a message for Clay from Sheriff Thurmond in Victoria. The message was short but to the point. Carl Krauss had been cornered at the ranch that he claimed he owned. A gunfight ensued, one deputy was wounded, and Krauss escaped and has not been seen since. Clay told Alice what the message said and told her not to worry. "Carl doesn't know where you are, so you have nothing to worry about as long as you stay here."

That night Willie Stanton came to the house and announced that he was on guard duty outside and not to shoot him without giving notice first. Alice thought that was funny and laughed out loud. That was the first time Clay had heard her laugh in all the time they had spent together. She went to the kitchen and got two cups of coffee and brought them into the dining room where Clay and Willie were talking and gave one cup to Willie and the other to Clay. She returned in a minute with a cup for herself, sat at the table with them, and joined their conversation. A little while later Clay noticed they were paying no attention to him but were engaged in a conversation of their own, so he took his coffee and went into the other room where Marilyn was playing with the baby daughter and Carter. He whispered to Marilyn, "Looks like we may have a new romance blooming in there."

"Wouldn't that be something? They both need someone. It isn't good to be alone, believe me, I know how that feels."

"You and me both." Clay said.

After a short while, they heard the front door open and close as Alice and Willie went out and took seats in the swing on the front porch. Clay and Marilyn snuck off to bed after putting the children to bed.

The next morning, Willie and Alice looked like neither of them had gotten any sleep. Alice came to the breakfast table looking like she was half asleep, and Willie was sacked out in the bunkhouse.

When asked what time she got to bed last night, Alice just smiled and said, "I don't know, I wasn't looking at the clock."

Clay and Marilyn laughed and dropped the subject.

Later that day, after lunch, when both had recovered from the night before, Willie took Alice for a ride around the ranch and showed her where he lived. He took her to Luke and Maddie's house and introduced her to Maddie and their children; there were three of them now, and then they went to Ed and Lisa's house and she met them and their children. As they were leaving there Alice remarked, "Y'all have your own little community here, and it looks like all of you get along great together."

Willie answered, "Yeah, we do. Clay, Ed, and I grew up together in Tennessee. When Clay came back from the war he found that everyone thought he was dead. His folks were dead, and his fiancé - thinking he was dead, had married another man. The carpetbaggers had stolen his farm, horses, and cattle, so he recruited several of us and we stole his cattle and horses back and sold them. That gave him the money to come here and start over. Ellen was Ed's little sister and she grew up with Clay, like the rest of us, but she was just a kid to us then. But boy, when she grew up, she grew up. She and Clay fell in love while we were driving the cattle to market and got married before we got home. We met Luke, who was working for one of the main thieves who were taking over most of the land in Tennessee when he came to our camp to kill us and take the horses back. It turned out he didn't like working for the other guys, so he joined us and helped us wipe them out. He ended up marrying my aunt Maddie. Actually, she was married to my dad's brother, which makes her my aunt by marriage, no blood kin. Her husband, my uncle, was killed during the war. She and Luke met during our fight with the carpetbagger's and got married the same time

Ed and Lisa did. That's another long story I'll have to tell you another time."

(Revenge Texas Style, Book 2)

They were just leaving Ed and Lisa's house when Willie spotted movement in the trees ahead of them. He immediately grabbed the bridle of Alice's horse and rode behind a large mesquite bush, pulled the rifle from the scabbard on his saddle, and told her to get down and stand between the horses. She did without asking any questions. She had noticed there was a rifle in the boot on her saddle, so she pulled it and jacked a round into the chamber. "What did you see?" She whispered.

"I don't know, just movement where there shouldn't be any."

"Where did you see it?" She asked.

"Look straight ahead and slightly to the left where that limb is hanging down from that big tree. It was right in there. I couldn't tell what it was, it could be a cow or a deer, but it may be something else. It's the something else we have to be concerned about. Let's just remain still for a while and see what happens."

Willie was standing behind the thickest part of the mesquite bush and looking around the side of it. The bush would not stop a bullet if someone shot at him but he had to be where he could see. He was about to think he had imagined seeing movement up there when he suddenly saw it again. He whispered to Alice, "There, see that, just to the right of that big tree. Looks like a man. There's another one to his left. They are watching Clay's house. You stay here and keep the horses quiet. I'm going to get closer and see if I can tell what they are up to. If shooting starts you get back to Ed and Lisa's and let them know what is happening, ok?"

"Ok, you be careful, you hear me?"

Willie looked the ground over carefully between him and the men and decided the best way to approach their position without being seen. He got down on his stomach and crawled to his left about fifty feet until he was behind some more thick brush. When he was hidden from their view he got to his feet and sprinted to the next place of cover. There he had to get down and crawl to the next cover. Eventually, he was close enough to recognize the men from the description Clay had given of Black Wolf. When Willie saw him, he realized just how big the man is. He then understood how the man could take three bullets to the chest and get up and walk away. He was determined if he had to shoot him he would shoot for the head. He didn't want that man coming after him, and he sure didn't want him coming after Alice. He had grown very fond of her in just the short time he had known her. He knew she had a husband, but thought that situation was going to be remedied soon.

During the time she had been staying with Clay and Marilyn, Alice had taken to the two children and took them everywhere she went around the place. Several times she had remarked to Marilyn that she wished she had children, but not if Carl was going to be their father. She didn't understand how she had not gotten pregnant by him, but she was so thankful that she hadn't.

Willie watched the men and discovered another man to Black Wolf's right. That made three that he knew of. They were all looking in the other direction so he felt safe for now to just observe. If they started to cause trouble he was in a good position to take two of them out before they even knew he was there. Black Wolf would be the first one to get his bullet if it came to that, and he was pretty sure it would, probably real soon. They were beginning to move closer to the edge of the trees closest to the house. As they moved forward, Willie crept closer also, always keeping Black Wolf in his sight. He didn't want to lose sight of him, no matter what else happened. By now Willie was only about thirty yards behind them and all three were in plain sight. They were taking positions behind trees and looked like they were about to shoot at something when Willie, concentrating on what they were doing, accidentally stepped on a dead tree branch. It sounded like a rifle shot in the stillness with the tension so high. Black Wolf and his men whirled about and saw Willie with his rifle pointed at them ready to fire. Before Willie could get off a shot, Black Wolf pulled the trigger and the bullet missed Willie by an inch as it skimmed by his left ear. He instinctively ducked and missed his shot. All four of the men, Willie, and the three Indians went to the ground and took cover. Willie wiggled back to where he could get behind a tree. When he looked around the trunk he could see nothing of the other three men. They were also hidden, and if he had to bet he would put his money on them trying to circle around and flank him on both sides. He immediately started working his way back toward the horses and Alice. He was hoping she had followed his instruction and was headed back to Ed's house. He continued to withdraw and remain as concealed as he could, which was not so easy. The underbrush was not all that thick here. He had to be very careful where he went. He discovered he had gone about as far as he could go without getting up and running across a wide opening. He wasn't ready to do that yet. He settled down in a thick bush with nothing else around it. The limbs were just inches off the ground and spread out over eight to ten feet. He crawled under the low limbs and remained perfectly still. His clothes blended with the brown and green shrubbery, so unless he moved, maybe they wouldn't see him until he saw them first. That was his only hope at this point. He had nowhere to go without exposing himself. He had been shot before and he didn't like it then, and he was sure he wouldn't like it now. Nothing was moving but his eyes. His rifle was out in front of him with the hammer at full cock. If he saw one of them all he had to do was shift the barrel of his rifle until the sights lined up on the target and pull the trigger.

He hadn't realized how hot it was until just now when sweat dripped into his eyes and off the end of his nose. He waited, watched, and listened. The longer he waited the tighter the tension grew. He wondered where Alice was. Did anyone at the house hear the shots? They had to have heard. They weren't over one hundred yards away. Someone would be coming to check at any time. That would put them in danger since they wouldn't know what they were up against. He had to keep his eyes open for them also. He couldn't allow them to walk into a trap and he didn't want to mistake his friends for enemies and shoot the wrong person. He also didn't want to be shot by one of his friends either.

The sweat was stinging his eyes so bad he slowly lifted his left arm and ran his sleeve across his face. He no more than lowered his hand back down to the stock of his rifle when a bullet hit the ground inches from his face sending all kinds of debris in his eyes blinding him for a moment until he could wipe his face and eyes. Meantime two more shots came very close while he was trying to see where they were coming from. Finally, he spotted a puff of gun smoke off to his right which made it harder for him to get his rifle around to make the shot. He had no choice but to make the effort. He whirled to his right, swinging the rifle around and bringing it in line just as another rifle fired farther to his right. His target suddenly fell from the bush thrashing about for a minute or so before it ceased to move. He quickly looked to his right to see where the shot came from and saw Alice standing where they had left the horses. Just as he saw her she darted back behind the bush and was hidden from his view. He couldn't keep from thinking to himself, "Now there's a woman for you."

That still left two of them out there somewhere. He swung back to his left assuming one in front and one to his left. At least that's what he would do if he was in their position. But these were Indians, so he didn't know how they thought.

He needed to make his way back to Alice, so he started scooting backward while keeping his eyes out in front of him to detect any movement. He was halfway across the opening when he saw one of the Indians stand up and take aim at him. He barely had time to swing his rifle and fire before the bullet plowed into the dirt in front of him. He heard a grunt and the man fall while he was jacking another round into the barrel ready to fire. The Indian was down and rolling around on the ground moaning and holding his stomach. Willie knew that had to hurt. Being gut-shot was supposed to be about the worst thing that can happen to a man or woman. Sometimes it can take hours to die. To make sure he didn't get up and continue the fight, Willie put him out of his misery with another shot to the head. That left only Black Wolf, and Willie had no idea where he was. Willie was still out in the open, so he jumped to his feet and sprinted as fast as he could to where Alice was waiting with the horses. Before he got there he heard her scream. He was running as hard as he could but it seemed like his feet were made of lead. They just wouldn't move fast enough. He still had a few yards to go when he heard a scuffle in front of him. As he rounded the bush Black Wolf was throwing Alice across a horse. Willie gave the last bit of speed he could muster and reached Black Wolf just as he lifted his foot to mount the horse behind Alice. Afraid of hitting Alice or the horse, Willie brought the butt of his rifle down across the back of Black Wolf's head as hard as he could swing it. He heard a loud crack and thought he had broken his rifle. He brought it back again and this time he used the barrel to crack the skull of Black Wolf. The black Indian fell to the ground with blood gushing from the back of his head. Not taking any chances on him surviving again he struck him two more times. Willie fell to his knees gasping for breath. He was kneeling there when he felt someone grab him around the neck and pull him against them. It took a moment for it to sink in that Alice was hugging and kissing him while she was crying and clinging to him as if her life depended on it. He slowly turned to her and put his arms around her and held her close. After he caught his breath he lifted her in his arms and carried her away from the bloody sight that was lying at their feet.

They were kneeling and holding each other when Clay, Ed, Luke, and Lefty came rushing up. They didn't need to ask any questions to know what had happened.

The first Alice and Willie knew anyone else was there was when Clay said, "Let's make sure this guy is dead this time." He went over and felt his neck for a pulse. He stood up and said, "I think old Willie did the job better than I did. Let's check the others."

The bodies were gathered up and buried in the graveyard out of sight of the house. It was reserved for those who came with the intent to harm those who lived here. There were no names on any of the markers, just a cross, and a number. The numbers told how many had been killed attacking the people at the ranch. Clay would report the attack and the killings to the sheriff of DeWitt County in Cuero. A lot of people would be happy to know that Black Wolf was finally underground.

Alice was a nervous wreck after coming so close to being kidnapped again. It took several days for her to get over the shock. Willie was around as much as possible and took her riding and showed her everything on the ranch. Most of that was just to spend time with her. She had never been courted before. Carl took her as a child bride under false pretenses and forced himself on her. She was enjoying this other side of life. When the subject of Carl came up she didn't want to talk about it.

Saturday night came and Willie informed her there was a dance in town and asked her to go with him. She didn't know what to say. She had never been asked to a dance, or anywhere else, for that matter. "I don't know how to dance. I've never danced before. I wouldn't know what to do."

"Perfect," Willie said, "I'll teach you. You'll have a ball. Trust me."

"Oh, Willie, I don't know, I'll be so embarrassed."

"You will be the prettiest girl there and you'll be so busy dancing you won't have time to be embarrassed."

"But I've never done it before."

"Then I'll get your first dance."

With the help of Marilyn and the rest of the guys, they convinced her to go. They arrived just as the band was taking the stage. They found a table near the dance floor and Willie went to get them a glass of punch. When he came back the band was playing and Alice was sitting there with a big smile on her face enjoying the new experience. After the dance floor got crowded, he took her hand and dragged her onto the floor. He showed her where to put her hands and said, "Just follow me, step when I step, and try to keep time with the beat of the music." It took her a few minutes to get the hang of it but in no time she was doing the waltz and the polka as good as anyone on the floor. As soon as they returned to their table Clay grabbed her and said "May I have this dance, Miss Alice?"

"Why certainly, Mr. Clay."

For the rest of the night, she hardly got a chance to sit down. Every man in the place wanted to dance with the prettiest girl there. Before the evening was half over she had to ask for a break to let her feet and legs rest, but she did it with a smile.

In the buggy on the way home, she couldn't stop talking about the good time she had. Clay and Marilyn with the two kids were in the front seat and Willie and Alice were in the back when Lefty rode up beside them and told Clay, "There's someone following us, Clay. He came out of the bushes after we passed and is following about a hundred yards back. What do you want us to do?"

Clay thought a moment and then said, "Keep an eye on him for the time being and let's see what he does. It may just be someone going home from the dance."

"Then why would he be hiding in the bush until we passed?"

"I can think of several reasons why he may have needed to go into the bush."

They continued on the way home for several more miles and the man was still back there. Lefty came up beside the buggy again and said to Clay, "I don't like it, Clay. It looks like he is following us to see where we are going. I think we need to find out who he is and why he's following us. There's a curve in the road up ahead. When we go around the curve Matt and I are gonna drop off into the bushes and wait for him. If he is what you say then we have no problem, but if he isn't then we don't need him following us home."

"Ok, be careful and don't do anything you don't have to do, ok?"

"Got it." Lefty dropped back with Matt and when they went around the bend and were out of sight of the man behind them they each turned their horses and rode into the bushes on the side of the road. When the man got even with them, Lefty spoke to him in a calm, easy voice, "Hold up right there for a minute, fellow." Before the words were out of Lefty's mouth the man put the spurs to his horse and darted ahead as fast as his horse could go for a hundred feet or so and cut to the left into the bushes and trees on the side of the road. It was too dark to see where he went and only a fool would follow someone like that in the dark. Just to get their message across, Lefty and Matt both pulled their revolvers and fired a couple of shots in the air over his head. They listened for a minute to make sure he kept going before they continued down the road. They could hear him crashing through the brush and tree limbs for a good minute. They laughed as they galloped up to the back of the buggy and told them what happened. "I'll bet he has scratches and bruises all over him from the beating he took going through that jungle."

Clay asked if they got a good enough look to recognize him if they saw him again.

Lefty laughed and said, "No he took off as soon as he heard my voice. All I could tell was he was tall, and riding what was probably a sorrel horse."

Alice asked in a shaky voice, "Do you think it could be Carl?"

Clay thought a minute and answered, "It could be. If we act like it is and be prepared then we won't be surprised if it is."

"How did he find us?"

"All he would have to do is ask around. Remember I told him who I was as soon as we got to your place."

"Yes, I remember. So what do we do now? I'm scared, Clay, I'm really scared."

"Don't you worry bout a thing; you're about as safe here as you will ever be anywhere. There are always a couple of men around the place. No one is going to get close to you without several of us around."

"That makes me feel a little better, but I'm still scared."

"I understand. That's got to be natural after what you have been through. Give it some time. Things will get better, I promise."

CHAPTER THIRTEEN

For the next week, things were quiet around the BAR W. Two men were always around where Alice was. To no one's surprise, Willie was almost certainly to be one of them. They took rides around the ranch and inspected cattle and fences, but there was always another man with a rifle nearby or trailing them within sight.

During the second week, after the fight with Black Wolf, Ed rode in late one afternoon and went straight to Clay. "Clay, I think we have a problem."

"Why, what's up?" Clay asked, looking around and giving Ed his full attention.

"I was riding in the north pasture about an hour ago up by the big grove of trees. A man rode out of there and high-tailed it to the west about as fast as his horse could run. I took a look in the trees and found where a horse had been tied for several days, from the looks of the droppings. After scouting around a bit I found where he had been waiting at the edge of the trees where he had a perfect view of the ranch here. There were cigarette butts all around showing he had been there for quite some time, probably several days. Didn't find where he had a fire, so he wasn't camped there, but he could have a camp somewhere close by. You think it might be that Carl fellow?"

"Yeah, that would be my guess."

"So what do you want to do? We can't let him set up there and spy on us. He could pick any of us off from there at any time with a high-powered rifle."

"Yeah, you got that right. So, it sounds like he's probably not staying there at night, right?"

"That's what it looks like to me," Ed said.

"It's late enough in the day now that he probably won't be back today. So let's all meet in the bunkhouse at supper time and lay out a plan to nab this guy."

"Ok, I'll spread the word."

When the men gathered in the kitchen of the bunkhouse that evening, Clay was there to explain the situation and get everyone's suggestions on the best way to handle it without anyone getting hurt.

After kicking it around for several minutes over their meal and coffee afterward, they all agreed on a plan.

By four o'clock tomorrow morning, two men would be waiting near the spot where the man had been spying from. They would not take horses with them so there would be none to alert the spy's horse as he approached. Knowing where he tied his horse and where he spied from gave them a big advantage unless he changed his method of operation after being discovered by Ed.

Clay went back to the house and told Alice what was going on. She got scared again and started crying. "I don't want anyone to get hurt because of me. I've been way too much trouble for y'all. I just need to go back to my place and deal with this myself."

"There's no way you're gonna do that," Marilyn said, "You wouldn't have a chance if he showed up with you there alone. He's already told you what he intends to do. How could you even consider going back there before he's out of the picture?"

"But I'm putting all of you in danger, especially the men that have to follow me around every time I step out the door."

"Alice, you are family here. We would do the same for any member of the family. In the short time that I've been here, I've come to know all these men. There is nothing that they can't handle. Just give them a couple of days and this will all be over. You wait and see."

"Ok, I hope you're right. But you have made me feel a lot better. I just don't want to see anyone get hurt on my account."

Marilyn hugged her and said, "Come on, help me get the kids ready for bed."

Alice picked up the baby girl, snuggled her to her chest, and said, "I love this little booger. I'm gonna steal you if your mamma doesn't watch it."

When the kids were tucked away in bed, the women returned to the dining room and had another cup of coffee before turning in.

The next morning, before anyone else was awake; Lefty and Willie were hidden in the trees waiting for the spy to return.

They waited until long after daylight when they decided he wasn't coming. They waited another hour and returned to the house.

Normal activities carried on for the next several days without any interruption. Lefty and Willie went to the lookout point for the first three days, but when no one showed up; they decided they had scared him away for now, and all agreed to give it a rest for a few days and see what happened. Alice was still kept close to the house, and two men went with her when she did need to get out for a little while.

"Marilyn, I feel like a prisoner here. I think I need to go back to my place and face whatever happens. I can't stay here forever depending on y'all to protect me and feed me. I'm even wearing your clothes, and this isn't right."

Marilyn came and sat at the table with her and said, "I can understand how you feel. Let's talk to Clay when he comes in and get his thoughts on it, ok?"

"I'm scared to go back there, but I can't stay here any longer. Maybe Willie will go with me."

"Oh, I'm pretty sure he will. You probably can't get away from here without him. But, if Carl is there when you get there, that's gonna put Willie in real danger when Carl sees you riding up with another man."

"Yes, I know, and I can't do that to Willie, he has been so sweet and helpful. I just wish I had met him before all this other mess happened. My life would have been so much different."

"That's all water under the bridge now. There's nothing we can do about the past, so let's concentrate on the future. What do you want to do when you get back home? I'm thinking maybe you should sell your place, take the money and start a new life. The only problem with that is Carl. You can't sell it without his signature. I guess that means somehow Carl has to be persuaded to sign the papers. Do you think he would do that?"

Alice was sitting at the table with a cup of cold coffee in front of her. She was nervous, wringing her hands and shaking, "No I don't. If he did he would want all the money since he claims he owns it and not me."

"Here comes Clay, let's see what he thinks."

When they explained to Clay that Alice wanted to go back to her place and bring this thing to a close one way or the other, Clay had to agree with her. "But we have to come up with a plan to make sure you don't get hurt." After thinking about it for a while Clay suggested that he ride into Cuero and talk to Sheriff Weisiger and see if he had any information on Carl. He knew the Sheriff of Victoria County had put out a wanted poster on him since he shot one of his deputies the last time they encountered him. "Maybe the two sheriffs have been in touch with each other. I'll ride in tomorrow and have a chat with him. We can decide how, when and what when I get back. How does that sound?"

"Ok, I guess," Alice said.

The next morning after the chores were done around the ranch, Clay saddled his horse and rode into Cuero. As he rode his mind was occupied with other things. He was not paying attention to anything around him, so when the hat flew off his head he didn't realize what had happened until he heard the shot. It took a moment to realize he had been shot at. He put his spurs to his horse, leaned as far to the side as he could, and raced away down the trail. When he went around a bend in the road a short distance away, he pulled his horse into the trees on the side of the road. He listened for a moment but didn't hear anything, so he slowly rode back toward where the shot came from but stayed off the road in the trees and brush. He took his time; with his revolver in his hand and his rifle loose in the holster. Every few seconds he pulled his horse to a stop and listened. He had covered maybe a hundred yards when he heard a horse moving through the trees. It sounded like it was moving away from him so he asked for a little more speed from his horse and got it. He knew they were making way too much noise, but he wanted to catch whoever it was that took a shot at him, so he kept pushing about as fast as he could go through the thick brush and trees that grew along the side of the road.

The next time he stopped to listen he didn't hear anything. Did that mean the shooter was already out of the area or was he waiting in ambush to get another shot at Clay? He couldn't take a chance on the man missing a second shot, so he dismounted and tied his horse to a bush, and advanced on foot as fast and quiet as he could. Every few steps he stopped to listen and look around. It was taking much longer than he wanted, but he would rather take the time than get shot again. That had happened too many times already and he wasn't looking forward to doing it again.

He continued slowly creeping through the underbrush until he came to the horse track left by the shooter. He knew they belonged to the shooter because they were still very fresh. He looked around as far as he could see which wasn't very far because of the thick brush. After satisfying himself there was no one else around he studied the tracks until he thought he would know them if he ever saw them again. He followed the tracks on foot far enough to assure him the shooter had left the area before he returned to his horse. After he was mounted he took up the trail again. He had no trouble following the tracks through the soft ground under the trees and brush. The rider didn't seem to be in a hurry, according to what he was reading from the tracks. Was he moving slowly because he was confident that he wasn't being followed, or was he trying not to make any noise? It didn't make any difference to Clay. The man was getting away, so Clay pushed his horse through the thick growth as fast as he could and still follow the tracks.

The growth was very thick along the banks of the Guadalupe River. The road from the Bar W ranch to Cuero followed the winding course of the river the entire way so there were many twists and turns in the ten-mile route. Eventually, the tracks led to the bank of the river and showed where the rider crossed. Clay crossed the river and followed the tracks until they became lost in a swampy area. With no track to follow Clay was at a loss to discover who took the shot at him. He was about to return to the road and continue to Cuero when he had another thought. These swampy areas usually were not too large, so the rider had to come out somewhere. Since the rider had been riding south this whole time Clay followed the edge of the swamp toward the south. He rode slow, watching the ground and also watching the surrounding area to try to avoid getting shot at again. The odds of him missing a second were not good enough for Clay.

He had ridden three-quarters of the way around the swamp when he found the tracks of the horse where he came out of the swamp. He took a minute or two to scan the area before he took up the trail again. The trail took a turn back toward the north, which would take him back toward the Bar W. When Clay realized that, and that the shooter had not tried to ambush him again after that one shot, he began pushing his horse for more speed. As long as he could see the track, which was not a problem since the ground under the trees was moist and soft, he kept up a pretty fast pace. The tracks wound in and out through the trees and swampy areas until they finally went into another swamp and just disappeared completely. As he had done before, he circled the edge of the swamp looking for tracks where he left the swamp. But after making a complete circle around the swamp and finding no tracks where anyone had left it, he was stumped. The only conclusion he could reach was the man must still be in there somewhere. He went in but he had not come out. At least he left no tracks if he came out, or did he just miss them? Clay retraced his steps, taking his time and being very careful not to miss anything along the way. It took him over an hour to completely circle the swampy area. If he was still in there Clay had no intention of going in there after him. That would be like going into a dark room looking for a cottonmouth moccasin snake. They give you no warning before they strike, not like a rattlesnake who will give you plenty of notice before they bite you.

After satisfying himself that the shooter had not left the swamp, Clay was torn between continuing to Cuero to talk to the sheriff and waiting around to see if the man left the swamp. After a few minutes of thought, he decided to wait a few minutes to see if he emerged.

Clay rode away back the way he came, hoping to make the shooter think he had left the area. After a couple of hundred yards, he circled back to where he thought the man would show himself if he kept on the same course he had been on for the last hour or so. He tied his horse back in the brush, and taking his rifle, he crept to where he could see the edge of the swamp for a hundred yards in each direction. Without exposing himself, he found a nice spot amongst low undergrowth where he had a good view and settled down to wait. This was the hardest part of tracking a criminal, the waiting, not knowing if or when or where he would show.

It seemed like it was always hot and muggy and flies were plentiful when he was in this situation. It brought back so many unpleasant memories that he almost got up and walked out. But he also knew if he didn't get the shooter now, he would have it to face at another time, which would be at the shooter's choosing. He forced the thought from his mind and concentrated on the task at hand.

It was so quiet and still, and so hot, that he was having trouble keeping his eyes open. He tried flexing his muscles without moving which would give his position away and possibly get him shot. That thought helped to keep him awake for a few minutes, and then he started to doze again.

After what seemed like two hours, probably not more than one hour, he gave up and slowly and quietly eased back to his horse. After listening a moment to be sure he wasn't followed, he mounted and rode straight away from the swamp and circled back to the road and picked up his hat, and rode on to Cuero.

The first place he went was the sheriff's office. No one was there so he went across and down the street to the saloon that was one of Sheriff Weisiger's hangouts when he wasn't busy doing sheriff stuff. Clay walked in and paused just inside the door to let his eyes adjust to the dim light inside. He spotted the sheriff sitting at a table with two other men that Clay recognized as local ranchers. He removed his hat and wound his way between the tables and other drinkers until he reached the sheriff's table. Sheriff Weisiger saw him coming and motioned for him to take a chair. "Howdy Clay, what brings you to town this time of day in the middle of the week?"

"Howdy Sheriff, gentlemen, looks like y'all are up to your elbows in a lot of nothing, must be a slow day in town."

The other two men spoke to Clay and confirmed his suspicions that nothing was going on.

Clay signaled for the bartender to bring him a beer and carried on small talk until it arrived.

The sheriff finally asked him, "What brings you to town Clay? I know you didn't ride all that distance just to have a beer with me, so what's on your mind?

"I was wondering if you have heard anything about Carl Krauss from over near Victoria. You know he is suspected of killing his wife's mom and dad and threatened to kill her. In fact, someone took a shot at me as I was riding in just now, and a man was spotted spying on the house a few days back. We set up an ambush for him but he never came back. Have you heard anything from Sheriff Thurmond?"

"Just what I told you the last time we talked. Since then I ain't heard a word about him. I don't think I would know him if he walked through that door right now."

"Yeah", Clay said, "and that could be a problem, although he has no reason to be holding a grudge against you, yet, but if you give him the time he'll find a reason. He's one disgruntled human being."

"I have a description of him, but it could fit half of the men in Cuero, so it's not much help," the sheriff said.

"I know what you mean. At least he's not gunning for you, so you don't have to be on your toes twenty-four hours of every-day expecting a bullet in the back with every breath you take. That gets very nerve-racking, you ought to try it some time."

Sheriff Weisiger and the other two men at the table laughed and the sheriff said, "No thank you, you seem to be handling that pretty good, so I'll leave that to you."

"I have a request; in an official capacity, could you send a telegram to Sheriff Thurmond and ask if he has any information on Krauss's whereabouts? You see, Ms. Taylor wants to go home. But as long as Krauss is running loose, it doesn't make sense to put her right in his hands."

"Yeah, sure I can do that, I don't guess the city council will gripe too much about the cost of a telegram. Walk with me over to the depot and we'll send it right now. You can wait around for a reply if you want, but I don't know how long it'll take to get it."

After the message was sent, Clay and the sheriff went to the diner for lunch. While they were eating a young boy, about twelve or so, came in with a message for the sheriff. The telegram said there had been no word or sighting of Krauss since the gunfight at the ranch.

"We'll, that doesn't help any." Clay remarked. "That could mean he has left the area, or he could be hiding out just waiting for the right opportunity to cause more trouble for Alice."

"Yeah, I see your point, Clay. So what are you gonna do? You can't let that little lady go home by herself. If he is waiting around for her to show up that would be letting her commit suicide."

"You're right, Sheriff. I guess a couple of men will have to go with her and stay until she can get things worked out. But, just between you and me, if things continue the way they are going between her and Willie Stanton she will probably be selling her place and moving out to the Bar W."

"That sounds promising, but what about her husband? They can't be getting too serious with him still in the picture."

"That does create a problem. But I just have a feeling that problem is going to take care of itself if he shows up around here."

"Now don't you go plotting a killing without just cause. That could get you in trouble with the law, and that means me."

"Oh, if it happens it'll be for just cause, believe me. So, I better be getting on back home."

"You be careful Clay, you don't want any more holes in that hat."

"Thanks for your concern about my hat, that's very touching."

Clay left the diner and headed home. As he left town and took the road that they always use he suddenly had an uneasy thought. "If that guy is waiting for me again, I'm making it too easy for him by riding this same road." He was not going to give him another shot and hope he missed again, so the first opportunity he got to leave the road he took it. He rode east about two hundred yards and then turned parallel to the road and continued while watching every bush and tree for a possible ambush. Having ridden this way many times over the years he knew just about every good ambush spot along the way. When approaching one of them he took his time and looked it over good before moving on. He knew he was taking an exceptionally long time to get home, but he figured it was better to get home upright than lying across his saddle.

He was within two miles of home, and about decided he was wasting his time being so cautious when his horse threw up his head and pricked his ears forward and to the left. Clay wasted no time in leaving the saddle. He went off on the right side, pulling his rifle from the boot as he slid to the ground. Once on the ground, he levered a round into the barrel and then remained perfectly still as he surveyed the area from under the horse's belly.

At this point, the road crossed the west edge of a small swampy area. No trees or brush grew in that area which made for a perfect ambush spot. That also meant the most logical place for the shooter would have to be on this side of the road which would put him very near where Clay was now. When he came to that conclusion, Clay started looking for the spot where he would be waiting if he was the one doing the ambushing. It didn't take long to spot a likely area. He slowly rose and removed the binoculars from the saddlebag and focused on that area. It only took a moment to detect a slight movement in the tree ahead and slightly to his left which was right at the edge of the trees on the east edge of the opening.

Clay had seen this many times in his life while hunting deer in Tennessee and chasing cows through the brush here in south Texas. Wild animals will skirt the edge of open areas like this rather than expose themselves, so there was a trail through the brush around the edge of the open swamp.

He waited a few more minutes, and when he was satisfied he had seen everything he was going to see, he slowly wrapped the bridle reins loosely around a small branch. If he should not be able to return the horse could work himself loose and go home.

He crept to his right as quietly as possible and then circled to his left until he was directly behind where he thought the shooter was hiding. He took another couple of minutes to look the area over. He didn't want to make the mistake of assuming his target was one place and find out the hard way that he was somewhere else. Just as he started moving forward a horse whinnied. Clay knew it was his horse and was ready when he was answered by another horse directly ahead of him. He waited but still didn't see anything until a horse and rider broke from the brush and went racing away. Clay got only a fleeting glimpse as they disappeared to the north. When he was sure the man was gone he went to where he saw him last and inspected the tracks. It only took a glance to recognize the tracks as the same ones he had seen earlier in the day when his hat was shot off his head not far from here.

Clay returned to his horse and followed the would-be dry-gulcher's tracks until he was sure he wasn't waiting to get another shot at him. But still, he took every precaution as he made his way home. There were no more incidents, but he was nervous as could be until he rode into the barn and dismounted.

CHAPTER FOURTEEN

Lefty saw him ride in and met him as he unsaddled his horse. "You look like you just came from the haunted woods. What happened?"

Clay smiled and answered, "You're right, I've been shot at and stalked until my nerves are shot."

Lefty walked closer and asked, "You were shot at? Where did this happen?"

Clay responded, "I was on my way to Cuero by that swamp on the right, a shot took my hat off and missed my head by less than an inch." Clay removed his hat and stuck his finger through the hole in the crown. "My hat can't take too many more of those."

Lefty, always the joker, said, "Maybe if you got a taller hat you would have a better chance of not getting hit."

"You do have a good idea there. Or, maybe I could get a smaller head."

"Why not do both?" asked Lefty.

Clay was smiling as he said, "The hat I can do, I don't know about the head size though."

The supper bell rang and all the crew headed for the bunk-house dining room while Clay went to the house and found supper waiting, along with Marilyn, Alice, Willie, and both of Clay and Marilyn's children. Marilyn and Alice wanted to know what took him so long to ride to Cuero and back. He didn't want to alarm them by talking about the shooting, but he couldn't see any way around it, so he told the story.

Alice asked, "Do you think it was Carl?"

"I didn't get a good enough look to make that determination, but I don't know of anyone else who has a reason to shoot at me. And, since this incident, I don't think it's a good idea for you to go home just yet."

"He's right Alice." Marilyn joined in, "It's too dangerous for you to even think about it."

"I know," said Alice, "But I'm worried sick just thinking about what he may be doing to my place. He could be selling off all the cattle and horses, burning down the house and barns, anything. He seems to have gone out of his head. There is no telling what he may do, or has already done while no one is around to stop him. I have to go. Willie, will you go with me?"

"Sure I will, I'm sure not going to let you go alone. Maybe Lefty will go too, the odds will be a lot better with the two of us if Carl is still around."

"Oh thank you, Willie, you don't know how much I appreciate you doing that."

"Ok, I'll go talk to Lefty and plan on leaving first thing in the morning, if that's ok with Clay."

"It's ok with me, but I sure wouldn't ride the usual routes, take a little extra time and do the unexpected, and be careful. Don't get careless and get shot. You won't like the experience. I can guarantee that."

"You don't have to tell me," Willie said, "remember, I've been there and done that."

"Yeah I remember, how could we forget, you remind us with that fake limp every chance you get."

"You're just jealous," as he exaggerated the limp leaving the room.

Lefty was happy to have something to do to get away from the ranch for a few days, so the next morning just as the sun was peeking over the trees the three of them were riding away from the Bar W heading for Cuero first, and then on to Victoria. They expected to reach Victoria just in time to take on a good meal and get a room at the hotel for the night. They didn't want to arrive at Alice's ranch in the dark of night, not knowing what they may encounter.

The timing worked out just as they planned. They were just finishing their meal when Sheriff Thurmond came in for his supper. He recognized Alice immediately and came over to say hello. She invited him to join them since she had a few questions she needed answers to.

When he was seated and had his coffee, and waiting on his food, she asked him about the story Carl had given her about people here in town talking about taking her ranch away from her because, at the time, she was only sixteen years old, underage and single.

"We'll, Alice, I never heard anything like that, and I'm sure if there had been talk about that I would have heard it. That obviously was something cooked up by Carl to scare you into marrying him."

"We'll it sure worked, and I've been paying for it ever since. He has made my life miserable. Have you seen him around here anywhere, or heard anything about him since I've been gone?"

"No, it's as if he just vanished from the face of the earth."

Willie chimed in, "I wouldn't say that. Someone has been spying on us at the ranch and someone took a shot at Clay just yesterday as he was riding to Cuero. Put a hole in his hat and missed him by an inch. We've never been able to get a good look at him, so we don't know who or why he's doing it. We are assuming it's Carl since we don't know anyone else who has a grudge against us. And, if it is him that would account for why you haven't seen anything of him around here."

"That makes sense, I guess." Sheriff Thurmond agreed.

Willie continued, "We'll be riding out to her place tomorrow morning, and we don't intend to take any flak from him if he's still around. Just so you know, we aren't going out there looking for trouble, but we are prepared to do what we have to do to keep Alice safe."

The sheriff scratched his head and took a sip of his coffee, "We have a warrant out for his arrest, so if you get the chance, you could bring him in and save me a lot of trouble tracking him down."

"From what I've heard, he isn't likely to lie down and surrender without a fight. I heard you had a run-in with him already that didn't turn out too good." Willie said with a smile.

"Yeah, he caught us by surprise, but that won't happen again. So if y'all run into trouble out there you let me know."

"If we run into trouble it'll be all over before you know about it, unless you ride out there with us, that is in your jurisdiction isn't it?"

"Yes, it is. Ok, I'll go with you. It might do me good to get out of town for a change. It can get awfully boring around here at times."

The sheriff's food came and Willie, Alice, and Lefty excused themselves and left for the hotel, hoping to get a good night's sleep. Lefty went to his and Willie's room and was asleep within minutes; however, Willie and Alice didn't get much sleep. It was early morning before Willie sneaked into bed without waking Lefty, he thought. Just as Willie thought he was safe, Lefty snickered and said, "I thought you wanted to get to bed early and get an early start tomorrow. Looks like you must have accomplished one of those goals." He snickered again and rolled over and, after a few more chuckles, went back to sleep.

At breakfast the next morning Willie and Alice were doing their best to avoid looking at each other until Lefty broke the silence when he asked Alice, "How did you sleep last night, Alice?"

Her face turned red and she glanced at Willie and said, "Ok, why do you ask?"

"We'll, Willie seemed to have trouble getting to sleep. He was up roaming the halls until early this morning. I thought he was never coming to bed."

Alice came back with, "And just what were you doing up so late that you know what he was doing?"

"Oh, I wasn't up at all. I was sleeping like a baby until he woke me up when he finally sneaked in just as the sun was coming up. Normally when a guy comes in that late he smells like a brewery, but he smelled of perfume, and… that's odd, it smelled a lot like that perfume you are wearing. Now I wonder how that could be."

Alice was still blushing but she wasn't about to let Lefty get the best of her. "Lefty, you know I am carrying a 44 in my pocket don't you? You best stop your wondering and turn your mind to something else before I decide to use it."

"Why Alice, I have no idea what you are talking about, I'm just concerned that you may not have gotten any more sleep than Willie did."

"Your concern is appreciated, but your health should be your first concern."

Lefty was enjoying joking with her, but he knew when to stop. "Your point is we'll taken. I'll not worry about your and Willie's sleep anymore."

Just as their food arrived at the table Sheriff Thurmond came in dressed for the trail.

The ride to Alice's ranch was uneventful until they got within sight of the place.

Sheriff Thurmond suggested they separate and come at it from two sides. "Alice, maybe you should wait back here until we make sure the place is safe."

"Ok, but y'all be careful, there is no telling what he'll do."

Sheriff Thurmond took the front, Willie and Lefty each rode to the left and right where they could cover both sides and the back of the house and the barns.

All three had their rifles in hand with a round in the chamber and their finger on the trigger expecting the worst.

When Sheriff Thurmond was fifty feet from the front door he stopped and dismounted and standing with his rifle across the saddle pointed toward the house he called out, "Hello the house, this is Sheriff Thurmond, I need to talk to you, come on out."

For what seemed like a very long time nothing happened, but then the front door opened and a man stepped out with a rifle in his hand. At the same time, there was movement at the curtain on the window to the left of the door.

The sheriff had never seen this man before, so he was taken aback for a moment.

"Who are you, I'm looking for Carl Krauss, is he here?"

"He's not here, what do you want him for?"

"Who are you?"

"I'm Slim Walker, I work here."

"Who hired you, Slim?"

"Mr. Krauss hired us. Why? Is something wrong?"

"There could be, do you know where he is?"

"No, he's been gone for over a week. Didn't say when he would be back."

"Slim, I need you to tell your friend inside at the window to put his gun down and come on outside. We aren't looking for any trouble with you, so don't bring it on yourself, and I'm not alone here, there are men on both sides and behind the house."

"I think you're bluffing, Sheriff."

"Look Slim, if you have nothing to hide what are you worried about? As I said, we aren't after you, so don't cause trouble for yourself. Come on out and let's talk."

"We got nothing to talk about Sheriff."

"You're making things look awfully suspicious Slim. What are you afraid of?"

While all this talk was taking place, Willie and Lefty were making their way to the back of the house. Lefty signaled to Willie that he would check the barn. Lefty signaled that he understood and got in a position to cover him if needed. Lefty quietly worked his way on foot to the side of the barn and peeked through a window. The interior was too dark to see much and he didn't want to have his head exposed in the window too long, so it was a quick look and duck down out of sight. He went to the other side of the window and did the same thing. There was another window farther along the wall, and after a quick look in there and still didn't see anything, he eased around the back corner of the barn. The double doors were open wide and he had a good view of the hall down the middle, but he couldn't see in the stalls and the hayloft above.

With chills running up and down his back, he stepped through the door and to the side with his back to the wall. He knew he made a good target if anyone was waiting in there, but he had to do it. After his eyes adjusted to the dim interior, he took a good look at everything he could see from there. After another minute, he took a deep breath and moved slowly along the hall, inspecting each stall and the loft as he did so. When he reached the front doors and had not gotten shot, or seen anything to cause alarm, he spotted Willie and signaled that all was clear. Willie then began his approach to the back of the house. There were curtains on all the windows, so he could see nothing through them, but he knew if anyone was inside they could see him when he passed in front of the window. With that in mind, he got down on his hands and knees and crawled under the windows until he reached the back door. It was closed so he waited and listened. The conversation between the two men out front was winding down and he knew he had to do something soon. He tried the doorknob and found it turned easily. When he pushed the door open with the barrel of his rifle it made no noise. He was thankful that someone had taken the time to oil the hinges. He waited a moment after the door was fully open before sticking his head around the door facing for just a second. When nothing happened, he took a longer look. He was looking into the kitchen and everything was a holy mess. Dirty dishes, pots and pans, and silverware were stacked everywhere. Flies were buzzing around the food scraps and having a feast. No one was in sight so he eased into the room and the first thing that hit him was the odor. Garbage was piled everywhere there was room for it. He made his way to the first door leading to the next room which he discovered was the dining and living room combined. The same scene was repeated there as in the kitchen, with dirty dishes, dirty clothes, and flies everywhere.

The conversation taking place in front was covering most of any noise he might make as he eased across the room to check out the rest of the house. When he reached the first door it was standing open, and when he peeked in he saw a man with a rifle looking out between the slightly parted curtains. Willie spoke softly to the man, "Put the rifle on the floor and don't turn around unless you want to die now."

The man whirled toward Willie bringing his rifle around with him, but just before he got it in line with Willie, he staggered back into the wall and slumped to the floor with a bullet in his chest and a shocked look on his dying face.

With nothing to worry about from this man, Willie quickly moved to the next door, and finding no one, he checked the rest of the house. When he was satisfied he was alone, he went to the front door and eased it open. Sheriff Thurmond still had his rifle aimed at the man who was standing with his back to the door. Willie told the man to put his rifle down or join his buddy in the graveyard. The man hesitated only a few seconds before putting his rifle on the floor. Willie then stepped out and lifted the revolver from the man's holster. "Now step back over here and sit on the floor, and don't give me an excuse to shoot you too."

Sheriff Thurmond tied his horse to the hitching post beside the house and stepped up on the porch. "Ok, Slim, I'm gonna ask you some questions and if I don't like the answers I'll take you back to Victoria and book you on suspicion of burglary, breaking and entering, and anything else I can think of. Here's the first question; where is Carl Krauss?"

"I already told you, I don't know. He left here over a week ago, didn't say when he would be back, and told us to make ourselves at home, which we did."

"Here's the second question; did he say where he was going or why he was going there?"

Slim hesitated a bit too long before he answered, "No, he didn't say."

Lefty walked up in time to hear that last answer, "This guy wouldn't know the truth if it bit him on the nose. Let me take him out behind the barn and shoot him and be done with it."

Sheriff Thurmond thought about it and said, "Why not? I'm thinking you're right, get him out of here."

Alice had heard the shot and then saw the men on the front porch talking, so she rode up just as Lefty was about to lead their captive away. She pointed and yelled, "That's one of the men that kidnapped me and dragged me halfway across Texas! Get out of the way, Sheriff, I'm gonna shoot that SOB!"

"Hold on Alice, we have more questions to ask this man now that we know that."

"You bet we do." She said, "and the first one is, did Carl Krauss put y'all up to that?"

"I don't know what you're talking about."

"Ok Slim, this is your last chance. Are you gonna answer our questions, or is Lefty gonna take you out behind the barn and shoot you?"

Slim sat there with his head down. After a minute Sheriff Thurmond told Lefty, "Ok Lefty, I'm gonna take a walk, there's something back up the road that I want to check out, and I don't want to see the man's face when I get back."

"Oh, you can be for sure THAT face won't be here when you get back. On your feet buddy, were going for a long walk."

"Now wait a minute, you can't do that, it ain't legal. You can't just shoot a man down in cold blood for no reason."

Willie grabbed Slim by the collar from one side and Lefty grabbed him from the other side and started walking him toward the barn. Alice fell in behind them determined to see Slim get what he had coming to him for what he had done to her.

They had just cleared the porch when Slim made a break, jerking away from Lefty and Willie and running as hard as he could toward the nearest patch of trees.

Lefty yelled, "Stop, you'll never make it Slim!"

But Slim was too afraid for his life to heed the warning. Just before he reached the first line of trees Alice stepped forward, raised her "44" and fired. Slim screamed and plunged forward on his face, doubled up in a ball holding his knee with blood squirting through his fingers. "You shot me, you shot me, you sorry ......"

"You're lucky she's a lousy shot," Willie joked, "she might have put that slug in the back of your head. How would you like that, Slim?"

The three of them walked up to Slim and looked down at him squirming around on the ground. Willie asked, "Should we leave him here to bleed to death or take him back to town and hang him?"

Alice pulled back the hammer on her revolver, aimed at his other knee, and said "I'll make sure he doesn't walk away before he dies."

Slim started screaming, "NO! Don't let her shoot me again, I'll tell you what you want to know, just don't let her shoot!"

Sheriff Thurmond rode up and wanted to know what was taking so long to dispose of this trash.

Lefty told him, "The clumsy oaf walked right in front of one of Alice's bullets."

Sheriff Thurmond laughed, "Maybe we should turn him over to her and not be bothered with taking him to town. He's gonna be hung anyway, what's the difference?"

"I like that idea, Sheriff," Alice said as she cocked the revolver again.

"No, no, I told you, I'll tell you anything you want to know!"

"Ok, answer the lady's question, did Carl Krauss hire you to kidnap his wife?"

Again, there was that long pause, "Yes, yes he did. He said if we made sure she didn't come back he would give us fifty head of cattle, with a bill of sale, so we could sell them. That would amount to over a thousand dollars. We didn't hurt her, we just did what we were gonna get paid to do."

Alice asked, "Did he give you the cattle?"

"No, when you came back he refused to deliver. He told us to wait here until he got back and if you showed up to make sure you didn't leave before he got back."

"And just what were you supposed to do with me until he got back?" She wanted to know.

"He didn't say."

"Alright, let's load him up and get on back to town." the Sheriff said.

"Before we go, Sheriff, I want to look around and see what they've done to my house."

Willie told her, "There's another body in there you may want to look at to see if he was involved in your kidnapping."

"Will you go with me?"

"Sure, come on."

Willie led her to the room where the man lay. When she saw him she covered her face and said, "Yes, he was the worst of them. I wish I was the one who shot him."

As she walked through the house she turned up her nose and commented, "How can anyone live like this? I feel like sticking a match to it and burning it. I never saw anything so filthy."

"That sounds like a good idea, but we can't do that. You have too much here to let it go up in flames. Why don't you ride back to town with the sheriff? Lefty and I'll stay here and clean this mess up, including that body."

"I can't let y'all do that, I'll stay and help."

"But what if Carl comes back while you're here?"

"I hope he does, I just hope he does."

"Ok, I'll drag this out and then I'll talk to the sheriff and Lefty and see what they think."

Willie took the dead man by the feet and dragged him out the back door, and across the yard, and out behind the barn where they would dig a hole and bury him. After talking the plan over with Lefty, the sheriff and his prisoner left for town.

The first thing they did was open all the doors and windows to let the place air out, and then it took over two hours for the three of them to haul the trash, dirty clothes, and other garbage outside. When all of it was in one pile they put a match to it and watched it burn.

Alice was busy inside scrubbing everything down with soap and water. When the men came back inside the place looked almost presentable. Alice's hair was wet with sweat and her face was red from the heat, but she was still beautiful to Willie. He walked up to her and put his arms around her from behind and hugged her close. She leaned back into him and sighed, "I've longed for someone to do that for such a long time, you have no idea how good that feels."

"We'll, young lady, you better get used to it, because unless you shoot me I plan to be doing this for a long time."

Alice turned around in his arms facing him, "Do you really mean that?"

"You bet I do."

She grabbed him around the neck and squeezed him so tight he could hardly breathe as she quietly cried on his shoulder. He held her until she cried herself out. When she relaxed and drew back to look him in the face he drew her close and kissed her long and sweet on the lips. She responded with all the passion she couldn't control.

They were like that when Lefty came in the door. "We'll excuse me; I didn't know there was a party going on."

Alice drew back from Willie just far enough to tell Lefty, "You are excused and you can leave now," and then she took up where she left off before he interrupted.

Lefty took the horses to the barn and unsaddled them and put them in stalls with feed, water, and oats. Then he spent the next hour brushing and rubbing them down while he kept a lookout. He didn't like the idea that Carl could ride in at any moment. He knew that would not be a pretty scene. But in a way, he hoped he did show up so they could put an end to this mess and get on with their lives. Alice didn't need to be saddled with that bum any longer.

Lefty ended up killing time in the barn and watching all the trails until right at sundown when Alice stuck her head out the door and called him to come in and eat.

When he walked into the kitchen he looked around and commented on the difference a woman's touch can make. "Willie, you need to take notice here. If you play your cards right you might get some help on learning how to keep house. Lord knows you sure need it. But when did y'all find time to cook and clean?"

Alice turned to face him with her hands on her hips, "Lefty Knox, you don't have any food yet, and if you plan on eating tonight you better watch your tongue. Do you get my drift?"

"Why Alice, I was only enquiring as to…"

"I know what you were implying", she interrupted.

Lefty hid his smile as he hung his hat on the rack by the door. "I see some changes coming around the Bar W."

"You're hopeless," she said as she placed the food on the table.

She had put together a very tasty meal, considering what she had to work with. They were finished eating and enjoying a final cup of coffee when Lefty said, "I think I'll sleep in the barn tonight. That way if we have any visitors we won't all get caught in one place. Besides, there will be too much noise in here for me to sleep anyway."

Alice whacked him across the head with her fist and said, "You're just jealous because you can't get a girl to even look at you."

"Why Alice, you don't know anything about my love life. Why that little gal at the bakery is just dying to spend some time with me. Too bad I have to work all the time or I'd probably be married by now."

Alice laughed out loud, "Lefty, that little girl at the baker, as you call her, is twice your size. If she got you in a bear hug there wouldn't be enough of you left to spread on a slice of bread."

"Aw, now Alice, that's not a very nice thing to say about that sweet little thing."

"I met that sweet little thing when I was in town, and if you think so much of her I'm gonna set you up with a date when we get home."

"Did you hear that Willie, she's already calling it home? You're in deep trouble boy."

"Yeah, that's the kind of trouble I like. Bring it on." Willie said happily.

Alice countered with, "I think Lefty may want to find another place to eat. His food may not be safe if he keeps up that kind of talk."

"I love your cooking, Alice. I apologize for everything I said if I offended you. You know I love having you around."

"You have an odd way of showing it."

"Aw Alice, I know you love me, you just have an odd way of showing it."

After a few more jabs back and forth with neither of them gaining an advantage, Lefty finally said, "I better head on out to the barn. You two love birds will want to get your rest, ha-ha."

Lefty rose from the table and took his hat from the rack by the door and left the house headed for the barn. When he stepped from the house onto the porch he quickly stepped to the side so he wouldn't be highlighted with the light behind him. He waited a few moments and then walked across the yard to the barn.

The interior was totally black when he reached the door. A chill ran down his back and he had second thoughts about walking through that door. Now he regretted not coming out here when there was enough light to see by. He stood outside the door for several minutes trying to decide if he really wanted to do this. While they were joking around and having fun inside, Carl, or anyone, could have slipped into the barn, and been waiting with open arms. It was not a reception he was looking forward to.

After a few more minutes of waiting and listening, he made up his mind to do it. He took a deep breath, drew his revolver, darted through the door and to the side, and put his back to the wall. He didn't realize how scared he was until he felt his heart racing. It felt like it would pop out of his chest at any moment. The tension was enough to make a wreck of a man's soul. He expected a bullet to come flying across the barn and bury into his chest at any moment.

He stood perfectly still, listening to every sound coming from the dark interior. His mind was picturing a man with a gun aimed at him ready to fire. After a few more minutes of this, he decided that sleeping in the barn was not a good idea. If someone was waiting in here they could remain still until he fell asleep and then have no trouble slitting his throat, and he would never know until it was too late. That was not a good thought.

He slowly eased back to the edge of the door, took a deep breath, and darted out along the side of the barn. He was in the shadow of the barn cast by the half-moon overhead. His bedroll was on his saddle in the barn, so he would have to make other arrangements for the night. With that thought, he moved away from the wall and made his way back to the house. He tapped lightly on the door and pulled it open and stepped inside to find a gun just inches from his face. A lamp was burning on the table nearby so he quickly recognized Willie holding the gun. "Why the warm welcome?"

"We'll, you didn't make a reservation, so you weren't expected."

"Sorry, I had a sudden change of mind about sleeping in the barn."

"Scared of the dark, huh?" Willie chuckled.

"Yeah, something like that. I saw a rat. Where is Alice?"

"She's in the back room getting a bath."

"If it's ok with you two I'll grab a blanket off one of the beds and sneak off in the woods. That barn is too likely a place to have unpleasant occupants. I'll take my chances elsewhere."

"You can sleep in the front room if you would rather."

At that moment Alice came in with a blanket wrapped around her shoulders and draped down to her feet. Her hair was washed and tied back into a bun on the back of her neck. Lefty knew she was Willie's girl but he couldn't keep from admiring her good looks and thought how lucky Willie was to have a girl like that.

"No, I think I better leave you two alone."

He nodded to Alice and went into the front bedroom and pulled a blanket from the bed and walked out the front door. He heard Alice ask, "Where is he going?"

"He's going to sleep outside so he can keep an eye on things in case we have any visitors."

Alice smiled and asked, "Does that mean we have the house to ourselves?"

"That's what it looks like. Do you have a problem with that?"

"Not if you don't."

He went around the house locking all the doors, there were only two, front and back. He checked the windows to make sure they were secure. He didn't want his night disturbed by an angry husband. When he came back into the living room Alice was sitting on the sofa with her feet tucked under the blanket looking like an angel.

Willie smiled and leaned over and blew out the lamp plunging the house into darkness. There was just enough light coming through the windows to show the way to the bedroom.

Lefty was bedded down snug and warm under a mesquite bush fifty feet from the side of the house when the light went out in the house. He smiled and said, You lucky devil."

He lay there in the dark listening to the night sounds until he drifted off to sleep. He awoke several times during the night and listened into the darkness, but the night passed quietly with no interruptions.

CHAPTER FIFTEEN

Lefty was awake the next morning before the day began to break. He lay in his blanket watching the sun light up the eastern sky until he had a good view of the house and barns. Nothing appeared out of the ordinary, but he waited until he heard movement in the house and a lamp was lit in the kitchen. Alice was probably getting ready to prepare breakfast and he should go in to see if she needed anything.

He took one last look around and threw back his blanket which was slightly damp from the dew that settled in overnight. He sat up and stretched to get the kinks out of his muscles and back. Something caught his attention off to his left near the back of the barn. He froze in the middle of rising from his blanket. His hand automatically went to the revolver on the blanket beside him. It slipped easily into his hand without him realizing it. Whatever he saw was too far away for a pistol shot, so he picked up his rifle and levered a round into the chamber. Keeping his eyes on the spot where he thought he saw the movement, he slowly swung the gun belt around his waist and buckled it. There was the movement again, but he could not distinguish what it was. He only got a glimpse of something brown. It could be a shirt or pants, maybe a buckskin shirt; it could be a cow or horse, it was too vague to be certain.

After waiting a long time to get a better idea of what he was up against, he started making his way through the trees to put the house between him and whatever it was out there. When he was sure he could not be seen he darted across the open yard to the front door and tapped lightly and waited for Willie to respond on the other side of the door. "Open up, it's me. We have a visitor."

The door swung open and Lefty went in and directly to a back window hoping to get a better look. Willie was at the other window looking where Lefty was pointing. "I didn't see enough to make out anything, just movement. It could be anything, but this is not a time to be taking chances."

Alice came in asking what was going on. Willie explained, and told her to stay away from windows, and don't open the doors until we know what we have.

There was occasional movement, but they still couldn't identify what it was.

The coffee was perking on the stove and Alice brought each of them a hot steaming cup. "You may as we'll be comfortable while you can. "How many eggs can you boys eat?"

Both answered at the same time, "I'll take four if you have enough. What do you have to go with them?"

She answered, "It looks like our previous guest ate all the bacon and ham, so it'll just be sourdough biscuits and honey."

"We've had a lot less many times." Lefty said, "Whatever you can put together will be fine."

Alice got busy preparing the sparse breakfast while the men kept watch. There was movement once in a while, but still, nothing to identify what it was. As they watched they became more certain that it was not a man. Anyone trying to hide and watch the house would not be moving that much. They talked it over and decided they had to go out and see what was there.

With rifles at the ready, they left the house by the front door and went into the woods out of sight of their intended objective. After entering the trees they went in opposite directions so they could approach from two sides. It took over thirty minutes to get to where they could start closing in on their prey. With guns loaded and ready they moved from tree to tree until they were within thirty yards of their target. A few feet farther and all their questions were answered. Hanging from a swaying branch was a brown shirt being moved gently by the breeze. Both men approached with guns ready, expecting some kind of trick. There were tracks made by large boots where the man had stood while attaching the shirt to the branch. Willie and Lefty were really confused now, until suddenly Willie said, "Alice," and broke into a sprint to the house. He hit the back door with Lefty right on his heels. Both came to a sudden stop and looked at the kitchen. Eggs were splattered across the floor and biscuits were burning in the oven, but there was no sign of Alice.

"Alice!" Willie screamed as he ran through the house. Lefty ran out the front door and spotted a cloud of dust far down the trail and going away fast.

"Willie, come here!" He yelled.

Willie ran out the door behind him, "What is it?"

Lefty pointed to the dust, "Get the horses!"

They made a mad dash for the barn. It only took four or five minutes to get their horses saddled, and they were racing down the road after the dust cloud. The horses were running wide open, but they didn't seem to be gaining much. Whoever had taken Alice had a big head start and the horses couldn't keep up this pace for very long. After a few minutes they realized this was not going to be a short run, so they eased the horses down into a comfortable ground-covering gallop. They could smell the dust but they were moving too fast to see any tracks. After another ten minutes or so the dust smell disappeared. Willie noticed it first and called for Lefty to stop. They searched the trail for tracks, but there were no fresh ones there. "They turned off somewhere back there." They wheeled their horses and headed back up the trail at a trot looking for where the horses, or horse, left the trail. It took only a couple of minutes to find it, but they had lost precious time, and there was no way they could make it up. There were tracks of only one horse. Lefty pointed that out to Willie and said, "That'll give us an advantage, with his horse carrying double he won't last long."

A few minutes later they lost the tracks again. They doubled back and located the trail, and saw where it took a ninety-degree turn to the right going into the thicker brush.

"I don't like this Willie, this brush is so thick he could be waiting within thirty feet and we can't see him until he has shot both of us."

"You are right, I'll follow their trail on foot and you bring up the rear with the horses. I won't be as easy a target on foot."

"No, that won't work. That game leg of yours is finally gonna come in handy for a change. You bring the horses; I can travel faster on foot than you can." He jumped off his horse and took off at a trot leaving his horse standing.

Willie picked up the reins and followed at a slower pace, but making sure he followed the tracks left by Lefty and the horse.

The tracks they were following took a sharp turn about every hundred yards in an attempt to throw them off the trail. But with Lefty on foot, the ruse was not working. When the trail took one of those sharp turns, Lefty would break a branch to alert Willie of the change in direction.

Lefty had to take his time and check every bush and tree because he didn't want to walk into an ambush. He had never had the experience of being shot, but he had seen several who were, and he didn't want to have that personal experience.

He moved as fast as he could through the brush and felt like he was probably making as good a time as the horse they were following, but he had no way of knowing for sure.

After a half-hour of traveling on foot, dodging brush and trees, going around deadfalls and broken limbs, Lefty was ready to let Willie take over. He gave it a few more minutes, and then he had to stop. He leaned against a tree and waited for Willie to catch up. He was gasping for breath when he said, "Ok, it's your turn, I've had it."

Willie gave the reins to Lefty and dismounted. "It doesn't look like he plans to ambush us. If he was, he would have done it by now, don't you think?"

"Maybe he's going to wait until his horse has played out, and then lay for us. He has to know we are following him unless he thinks he has thrown us off his trail with all the twists and turns he has made."

Willie was walking with Lefty riding beside him while they reviewed what they were thinking and what they knew.

Lefty pointed out, "Have you noticed anything about the direction he's going?"

Willie thought for a moment, "I hadn't noticed, but it looks like he is keeping to a northwest direction unless I've gotten turned around."

"I think you're right, even with all the turns he's making he always comes back to the same northwest direction. So what is northwest of here?"

"I don't know, I'm too new here," Willie said.

After a few minutes of thought, "Meyersville; there's a little settlement about twenty miles or so in that direction. A German fellow by the name of Meyers settled there about thirty years back. Hey, I just thought of something, Krauss is German ain't it?"

"Yeah, I think it is, what's on your mind?"

"That town was settled by Germans, Krauss is German, I think were on to something. I'll bet that's where he's from and that's where he's going. What do you want to bet?"

"That sounds too logical for me to bet against it. So what do you want to do?" Willie asked.

After some thought Lefty said, "What do you think about one of us going on to Meyersville and watching for anyone riding in with a pretty redhead in tow, while the other one stays on this trail, just in case he doesn't go to Meyersville?"

Willie thought about that a moment and said, "I don't think too much of that idea. The one following is in too much danger of being ambushed. And being alone he wouldn't stand much of a chance. With two of us, he probably would think twice before taking a shot at us. And, another thing, now that we think we know where he's headed if we should lose his trail we can still go to Meyersville and find him, or wait for him."

"Ok, that's the plan then," agreed Lefty, "let's go."

Willie mounted his horse and, with both riding, they made good time, but still took the precaution of checking all the places that looked like a good place to stage an ambush.

The trail eventually straightened out and stopped the crooked zigzag that he had been using since the chase began. When Lefty noticed there had been no changes in direction for quite some time he mentioned it to Willie, "It looks like he has made up his mind to head straight for where he's going. No more crooked trails. Let's pick up the pace a little, maybe we can catch up to him before he hits town, if that's where he's going."

They put their horses in a fast trot, alternating with a slow gallop, from time to time, where the trail would allow it.

After another hour, Willie remarked that the tracks were so fresh they can't be very far ahead.

Lefty agreed, but they kept up the fast pace hoping to catch a glimpse of them before they hit town.

As the sun was setting and the evening breeze picked up, they intersected a well-used wagon road going their direction. The tracks merged onto the road and continued northwest. But the closer they got to the town, the harder it got to distinguish

Alice's tracks from the others on the road. There hadn't been that much recent traffic, so with a little extra care and time, they were able to follow the tracks to the edge of town and see where they veered off to the north to avoid going into town.

"You see that?" Lefty asked, "He knows where he's going. I'll bet he has relatives here who will put him up until he decides what he's gonna do with Alice."

Willie agreed, and said, "I don't think he will know either of us unless he was watching us back at the house before he took Alice. Now that I've said that, he had to have been watching to set up that trap, and knew we would leave her alone to check it out."

"I'm sure you're right." Lefty pulled his horse to a stop with Willie stopping beside him.

"What are you doing?" Willie asked.

"I was just thinking, this place is not that big, but if he sees us riding down the street following him, he will either run or shoot us. If I had my druthers I'd prefer he run, I don't like being shot at. So here is what I'm thinking. We stable our horses, get a change of clothes and a different hat, and follow these tracks on foot. We could pretend to be a couple of drunks. That might be fun, don't you think? Heck, we might even get drunk, so we can pull it off good."

Willie chuckled and said, "Did anyone ever tell you you're crazy?"

"Oh, only a few times."

"Ok, if that's the best plan you can come up with let's do it. Where do we stable our horses?"

"I've only been here once a long time ago when I was just a kid, but I think there's a livery stable on the next street over if it's still there."

They found the livery stable right where Lefty remembered it to be. They led their horses in and made arrangements to board them for the night. "Where is a good place to eat and sleep in this town?" Lefty asked the young kid who was taking care of their horses.

"We'll, the best place to eat is Lizzies, on the main street. As far as a place to sleep, there ain't a hotel or anything like that. Most people who come here come to stay with kinfolks, or they sleep in the loft up there," as he pointed above his head.

They were leaving and heading for the door when Willie suddenly stopped and turned back and almost bumped into Lefty, "Speaking of kinfolks, do you know the Krauss family that lives here?"

"Do I, are you kin to them?"

"Just friends of the family, can you point out which house they live in?"

"I sure can, come over here." They walked outside and the kid pointed down the street, "See that house over there, with the white picket fence and the flowers in front?"

He was pointing to the fourth house on the left.

"Yeah, so that's where the Krauss's live? Do you know Carl?"

"Yeah I know Carl, in fact, you just missed him and his wife, that's his horse right there, they just rode in a few minutes ahead of you."

"We'll dang, I'm sorry we missed him. Did they go to the house over there?"

"Yeah, they sure did."

"I'm sure we'll catch up to him later then. You said he has a wife?"

"Yeah, prettiest girl I ever did see. But she must have been having a bad day because she looked like she didn't feel good at all."

"What do you mean?"

"Her eyes were all red like she had been crying a lot and she had a bad bruise on her cheek like she must have had a fall or something."

"Yeah she did, we heard she recently lost her mom. She's taking it pretty hard."

"Oh, by the way," Willie continued, "If you see them again don't mention you saw us, we want to surprise them. They don't know we are coming."

"Ok," he whispered, "I won't tell a soul." He snickered and went to shoveling horse manure.

Willie and Lefty left the livery feeling pretty proud.

As they were walking away in the opposite direction of the Krauss house, Lefty poked Willie with his elbow and said, "Willie, I think you should be a detective. Why we ain't been in town for five minutes and you already know everything we came here for."

"Maybe so, but maybe not, we still have no idea what Carl Krauss looks like. But he'll know us if he sees us walking down the street. He could walk right up to our face and put a bullet in both of us before we could blink an eye."

"Now why did you have to remind me of that? And I was feeling so good about everything."

"We'll, Lefty, you need to look on the bright side."

"What is the bright side of getting shot?"

Willie laughed and said, "He might miss."

Then Lefty laughed and said, "Or maybe he will shoot you first with his last bullet."

As they entered the main street they saw a general store right ahead. Lefty stopped and turned to Willie, "Do you have any money on you?"

"Some, why do you ask?"

"Remember, we were going to get a change of clothes, and that takes money."

Willie looked each of them up and down, "I think we can get by with just a new shirt and a hat. Our pants look like what everyone else is wearing, so he won't notice that."

Willie dug in his pockets and came up with thirteen dollars. "That ought to be enough if you don't want a tuxedo."

"You cheapskate."

"Ok, the next time we need clothes you can buy."

They were able to find everything they needed in the way of clothes. The hats left a lot to be desired, but they got what they could afford. The hats fit the description of drunks when they turned the brim down on one side and up on the other. As they walked from the store they looked at each other and laughed.

Lizzies turned out to be a good place to eat. But, they had not eaten since the night before so almost anything would have tasted good.

They took their time over dessert and coffee while watching the sunset. When it was dark enough for what they had planned, they paid for the meal and left the diner.

They strolled by the livery stable and peeked inside. No one was around at the moment, so they checked to see if the horse belonging to Carl Krauss was still there. He was, so they assumed Krauss was still at the house pointed out to them earlier. To further implement their plan they saddled their horses, and the one belonging to Krauss. When that was done they removed the three horses from their stalls and led them down the street and tied them in front of the house across the street from the Krauss home. They watched the house for a few minutes and saw no activity, so they approached the house and eased up to the window that was showing the most light. Curtains covered the window and blocked their view of the inside. Moving quietly around the house the rest of the windows were checked with the same results. With no knowledge of what the inside of the house looked like, or where the people inside might be, they were left with more decisions to make. They moved away from the house where they could talk without alerting the people inside.

"We'll, what do we do now?" Willie asked.

"Why are you asking me, that's your girl in there?"

"So you're gonna make me make all the decisions?"

"If we get killed doing this I don't want it to be my fault."

"Lefty, you're a lot of help."

"Thank you, I do my best."

"Do you have any ideas how to go about getting her out of there?"

"I like the drunken act, myself, what do you think?"

"It's as good as anything I've come up with. How do you want to do it?"

"How bout we come down the street singing like two drunks who got the wrong house. We just open the door and walk in singing and staggering. If the door is locked we knock and yell like drunks until it's opened. When it opens we stagger in to do what we have to, just play it by ear from there."

"But we don't even know if she's in there, Lefty. We could break in there and get shot for nothing."

"Ok, you go in first."

"What good is that gonna do?"

"I'll have my gun out ready to shoot if they shoot you."

"Thanks a lot. So after I'm dead what are you gonna do?"

"I'll apologize for the intrusion, take your girl and leave."

"Ok, Lefty, let's get serious here. How much of what you said is really what you want to do?"

"I guess everything except letting you get shot."

"Ok, let's do it, but if I get killed I'll never speak to you again."

"Fair enough, Willie, let's go."

They checked their revolvers and made sure they were loaded with six rounds, and then they ruffled up their clothes to look like they had slept in a barn and took to the street in front of the house. They put their arms around each other and sang at the top of their voice while staggering up the walk and onto the porch. They were both singing different songs, and then they stopped and laughed and started over. When they reached the door and turned the handle as if they belonged there it was locked. Both banged on the door and yelled, "Hey Bob, Joe, open up, we got your whisky."

It only took half a minute until the door was jerked open and they barged in, still singing at the top of their voice. When they didn't recognize the older man who opened the door they kept moving into the next room just like they lived there. The old man was trying to stop them, but they were paying no attention and kept moving through, forcing the old man along with them, first one room and then the next. They soon realized the old man was the only one here. All the time they were asking "Where are Joe and Bob, hey Joe, where are you?" When they reached a door that was locked they kicked it open and staggered in with their guns drawn. Sitting on the bed was Alice with her hands tied to the headboard and a gag in her mouth. The drunken act was dropped and Lefty turned to the old man and told him to stand still and he won't get hurt. Willie was busy cutting the ropes holding Alice, and before anyone could stop them they were out the door and heading for the horses. Lefty was walking backward covering the house while Willie was getting Alice on her horse and mounting his. When he was mounted he covered the house while Lefty mounted and they raced out of town without a shot being fired.

They raced the horses for a mile before they slowed down. When they were walking the horses side by side Willie asked Alice if she was alright.

"Yes, I am now, but I was worried half to death that you wouldn't be able to find me. How did you do that? And what was that drunken act back there?"

Lefty laughed and asked, "Did you like that?"

"That was the worst singing I have ever heard."

"How many drunks have you heard sing?"

"None half as bad as you two."

Willie asked, "Where was Carl when we broke in there?"

"He and a couple of friends of his went out drinking."

"What did he tell the old man about you?"

"He told him I was tired and was sleeping and not to disturb me. That old man knew nothing about what was going on."

"I'm glad we didn't hurt him then."

Lefty said, "We need to get off this road and find a place to settle down for the rest of the night. By my calculation, Cuero should be about due east from here. So if we keep going in that direction we can probably be there by noon tomorrow, if we get an early start in the morning. How does that sound to y'all?"

Alice said, "The part about finding a place for the rest of the night sounds like heaven to me."

"Ok, the moon is over there, so east should be that direction, follow me."

They were cutting across the country that none of them knew hoping no one would find their trail. They figured a tracker wouldn't be able to do anything until after daylight tomorrow, so they rode until they found a likely spot to camp. When they called a halt the horses were unsaddled and tied to trees. Bedrolls were thrown on the ground and everyone was sacked out in a few minutes. They were so tired they didn't even think about starting a fire.

They were up before sunrise and had a fire going with the coffee pot perking when Willie and Alice untangled from each other and sat up.

"That coffee smells so good. I hope it tastes as good as it smells."

"Alice, if you had ever tasted my coffee you know that is not gonna happen. I've been told I make the worst coffee of anyone."

"I won't believe that until I taste it."

CHAPTER SIXTEEN

They reached the Bar W ranch shortly after noon. When Marilyn heard what Alice had been through she took her directly to her bedroom and told her to lie down and rest while she prepared a good hot bath for her. When the bathwater was ready she notified Alice. While she was getting her bath Marilyn picked out one of her nicer dresses, along with all the undergarments, and had them laid out waiting for her. Alice got dressed and came to the dining room where Marilyn had a big bowl of beef stew, hot coffee, a wedge of cornbread, and a slice of cake waiting for her. Alice looked at the food and said, "With service like this I may arrange to get kidnapped more often."

When she finished eating Marilyn insisted she go to bed and get some rest.

Lefty and Willie had gone to the bunkhouse and had Wally fix them a meal with lots of coffee, after which they took to their bunks and didn't come out until morning.

Clay and Carter came in from the range and got the story from Marilyn. He sat thinking for a long time just shaking his head. Finally, Marilyn asks him what he was thinking, "I'm thinking that Carl is gonna come looking for Alice, and when he does there's gonna be trouble. But I don't think he will do it out in the open. He'll sneak around until he gets a clean shot at her, or someone else, most likely me, because I'm the only one he knows by sight unless he would recognize Willie or Lefty. And, this is probably the first place he'll come, so he could show up at any time."

With that thought, he got up from the table, strapped on his six-shooter, took his rifle down from over the door, and headed for the bunkhouse. Lefty and Willie were still sleeping, but since it was almost supper time, he shook both of them awake, "We need to talk."

They sat up, stretched and Lefty asked, "Is it morning already?"

Clay said, "Yeah, you've been asleep almost fifteen hours, I thought y'all were dead."

Lefty looked out the door and then out the window and said, "Naw, that can't be right, the sun is on the wrong side of the world if it is, what's up Clay?"

"Carl Krauss is what's up. I'm afraid he's gonna come gunnin' for Alice, and if he can't get a shot at her he'll probably shoot anyone he sees. What do y'all think?"

Willie was still rubbing the sleep out of his eyes when he said, "I have to agree with you. After the way he treated her yesterday, I wouldn't be a bit surprised at anything he does. The man is either crazy or so determined to get her ranch that he'll stop at nothing."

"I think he's right," Lefty said.

"In that case, we need to make some plans. It looks like we will need to keep a guard on the place day and night until he's put out of commission."

Willie got out of bed and started putting his boots on, "I'll ride over and tell Luke and Ed so they can help out."

Clay stood up to leave, "No, you get your rest, I'll go. We'll all need all the rest we can get before this is over."

"Thanks, Clay."

"Hey, don't mention it. I'm just wanting to give Alice a fighting chance to get your life straightened out. You don't seem to be doing a very good job of it."

"I didn't know it showed."

Clay returned later and told them Ed and Luke would be over later to take the night shift, and then Clay, Willie, and Lefty would take tomorrow and tomorrow night.

For the next three days, all was quiet at the Bar W ranch. The longer it remained that way the tighter everyone's nerves became. By the third night, they were jumping at the slightest sound. The place looked like an armed fortress with everyone, including the women, wearing sidearms and keeping a rifle or shotgun within reach. During the day the men took turns riding the perimeter of the home ranch. At night the patrols were pulled in closer to the house and barns with two men on guard at all times.

Clay slept in two-hour shifts when he could, and he was pretty sure most of the men, and women, were having the same problem sleeping. Everyone's nerves were on edge and occasionally sharp words were spoken over the slightest thing, and then they apologized and things were back as usual.

When the fourth day broke, Clay joined the men in the bunkhouse for a war council. Luke and Ed were there for a change. They usually took their meals at home with their wife and children, but they had just come off guard duty so this was the best time to catch everyone together.

When everyone had their food Clay asked, "Are y'all enjoying this new schedule?"

There were a few chuckles but overall no one said yes.

"I think Mr. Krauss is just waiting until we get tired of this game and relax our guard. So I'm thinking we need to take the fight to him. Lefty and Willie know where his relatives live in Meyersville, which is about twenty miles or so west of here. I think if we scout the most logical route between here and there we can probably pick up his trail if he's even doing what we think he's doing. He may not be giving us a second thought, but I have a hard time believing that. As long as Alice is around his life is in danger, because she is the only one who can testify against him if he should go on trial for murdering her folks. If she is eliminated he has total ownership of the ranch. That seems to be what he's really after, and she stands in his way, so she has to go."

"There are two things I think she needs to do. Number one is to go to Cuero, hire a lawyer, and file for divorce. Number two is to take back her ranch. The way it is now anyone could claim she has abandoned it and just take over. She probably could get it back, but it would take a lawsuit, and a judge's ruling, to do it. So, the easiest thing will be to move back to the ranch. She doesn't have to be there as long as someone is living there representing her. So, what do y'all think?"

Willie was the first to speak, "We'll, I'll certainly go."

Clay smiled, "I thought you would. Does anyone else want to go along with Willie and occupy Alice's ranch? He shouldn't be there alone with this guy gunning for anyone who gets in his way."

"I'll go if you don't need me here for anything."

"Thanks, Lefty, we'll manage to get by until this is settled. But y'all be careful. We don't want anyone getting hurt, especially someone on our team."

"Ok, we'll leave first thing in the morning."

Clay continued, "Matt, since you're the best tracker, if you want to get out and stretch your legs, how about you and Gerald see if you can pick up a sign of where he's been spying on us and follow it to see where it goes. If you find yourself in Meyersville check with that kid at the livery and see if Carl Krauss is still around. If he's not there try to find out how long he's been gone and if anyone else left with him. You think you can do that?"

Matt said, "We'll do our best, but we can't promise anything."

"That's all anyone can ask. Can y'all be ready to start in the morning?"

When everyone knew when and what they were expected to do Clay returned to the house and informed Alice of their plans.

"But I should be going with them to my place."

Clay reminded her, "But you and I will be going to the lawyer in Cuero to file for your divorce if you still want to do that."

"You bet I still want to do that. I should have done it a long time ago."

John Williams, who acted as Segundo when Clay was not around, would take the watch the first part of the night. He would be relieved by Romeo Sanchez, a new man who had only been with them a couple of months. He had proven to be the best horse wrangler and bronc rider among them. When he put the saddle on a young wild horse everyone stopped what they were doing to watch. He had a magic touch with horses, and it appeared that they understood when he talked to them.

The next morning everyone was up early getting ready to head out on their assigned task when John Williams stuck his head in the back door of the house and informed Clay that Romeo had not come in from his guard duty and didn't answer when they called him.

"That doesn't sound good. Get a couple of the boys and start searching where he was supposed to be. I'll be along as soon as I get my guns."

John returned to the bunkhouse and in a few minutes had everyone out looking for Romeo. They spread out in pairs, going in opposite directions. They all had guns in their hands and were expecting and prepared for the worst when Gerald called from the far side of the house.

Clay was just coming out the back door when he heard Gerald call, so he rushed in that direction. He found Gerald squatting on the ground looking at scuff marks and drops of blood on the leaves and ground.

"What you got, Gerald?" Clay asked as the others gathered around.

"So far just blood and tracks that I can't make heads or tails of. Maybe Matt can make some sense out of it."

Matt stepped forward and asked everyone to move back and don't disturb anything. He took a long time going over the entire area. When he was finally satisfied that he had seen everything, he returned to the group and told them what he suspected, based on the evidence that he saw.

"It looks like he was coming along here, probably in the dark, when someone jumped him from behind that tree. They had probably figured out his pattern and were waiting for him. From the amount of blood, it doesn't look like he was hurt too bad, but you never can tell for sure. He was dragged over there where someone else joined the first man, and they carried him to a horse on the other side of the hill. The horses then went off toward the river. That's as far as I got."

Clay looked around the group and pointed his finger, "Willie, Leftie, y'all go with Matt and follow this trail. How long do you think they've been gone, Matt?"

"It's hard to tell for sure, but I would guess it was shortly after he came on duty last night. This blood is almost dry. That would take several hours."

"So that could be as much as a six-hour head start."

"Yeah, that's about what I figure."

"I guess there's no use being in a big hurry now. They are probably already where they are headed, so y'all go ahead and eat your breakfast. John and Gerald, can y'all get their horses ready for them while they eat?"

"Sure can, come on John."

Clay returned to the house and informed the women of what was happening. When Alice heard that Willie and Lefty were going to her place she insisted on going with them. Clay was not in favor of that, but it was her choice. That's where she was when she was kidnapped, and the reason for going there was still the same.

He went to the barn and told them to saddle another horse for Alice. When he returned he said to Alice, "I'll ride with you as far as Cuero and the lawyer's office so you can file your divorce papers, and then y'all can go on from there. How does that sound?"

"Sounds good, I'll be so glad to get that over with."

Matt poked his head in the door and said, "Rider coming, Clay."

Clay went to the front door while Matt went around the house and was waiting at the corner when the rider stopped out front.

Clay stepped out onto the porch, "Can I help you with something?"

The man looked rather young, dressed like a poor farmer with overalls and a flop hat. The horse he was riding matched its rider and looked like it couldn't go much farther.

"I have a message here for Clay Wade. Would that be you?"

"Yes, that's me, who's the message from?"

"I don't rightly know his name. He just said to give this message to you." As he removed a slip of paper from his pocket and extended it to Clay.

Clay stepped off the porch and retrieved the message, unfolded the paper, and read it.

"Have the girl at the big white rock on the river at sundown or your man dies."

Clay read it again and asked, "Who gave you this?"

"I done told you I don't know his name."

"Where were you when he gave it to you?"

"I was in town when he came up to me, gave me a dollar, and told me to deliver it to you."

"What town was this?"

"Meyersville, that's where I live."

"Was that mans name Carl Krauss?"

"Yeah, that's it. I couldn't think of it until you said it. I've seen him around town but I don't know him. He hangs out with a pretty rough bunch."

"Do you know how many are in that bunch?"

"There could be as many as six, maybe more."

"By the way, what is your name?"

"They call me Sunny. Ma said it's because of my sunny personality, whatever that is."

"Ok Sunny, thanks for bringing the message, are you supposed to take an answer back to him?"

"Naw, he didn't say so."

"Ok, thanks, do you need to water your horse?"

"Naw, he just drank at the river, he's full."

Clay gave him a half-hearted salute and watched him ride away. From the position of the sun, he could tell it was about mid-day. That gave them about six hours to decide what to do and get it done.

"Call all the men together Matt, we need to talk."

"Yes sir." Matt trotted back to the barn where the horses were being saddled.

Clay went inside and told Marilyn and Alice what was going on.

When Alice heard what Carl was pulling, she said she would be ready to ride when they were.

"Wait a minute there, you aren't going anywhere."

"Clay, I'm not going to let that young man die because of me."

"There has to be another way. We will come up with something, just give me a few minutes, but there is no way we are going to turn you over to them, so forget about it."

Clay left the house to meet with the men at the bunkhouse. When he entered the door he discovered Alice was right behind him.

"You're not going anywhere without me," she said.

He explained the note and the situation and asked if anyone had any ideas.

They all started talking amongst themselves and everyone had thoughts on the subject but no one could come up with a plan that they could all agree on.

Clay was trying to take in what everyone was saying, but too many were talking at once. Finally, he asked for quiet and started at one end of the table and pointed a finger at Luke, "Do you have any thought as to how we might handle this, Luke?"

"My thought would be to get there long before they do and be waiting for them and don't give them a chance to get set up."

"That sounds like a good plan to me." Clay said, "Does anyone else have a suggestion?"

John held up his hand, "We still have about five or six hours before sundown. Maybe we can track them from where they ambushed Romeo and attack them before they even head for the meeting place."

"That would be even better than waiting for them. Matt, do you think you can follow their trail?"

"If they don't do something tricky to cover their tracks, I should be able to."

Clay looked around the table and asked if anyone else had anything to say. They all shook their heads, so he said, "Ok, get saddled up, Matt will lead out, we will follow at a safe distance. If we haven't found them by, say four o'clock, we'll head back to the meeting place and wait for them there. How does that sound?"

No one had any objections, but before they could leave Clay cautioned them, "Just a minute men. If we get a chance to ambush them, just be careful and don't shoot Romeo."

Lefty, always the joker, said, "Yeah, that would be a good joke on him, wouldn't it?"

The horses were saddled and everyone was ready to ride in ten minutes. Clay told Alice she should stay here since they were not going to meet the kidnappers just now. She finally agreed and went back to the house.

Then Clay told them, "Someone needs to stay here in case those guys come here while we've all gone to meet them."

Since Alice was staying behind Willie agreed to stay and guard the place.

Lefty spoke up, "I can see it now, only one person is going to have a guard, and a marching band could sneak up on them and they would never know it."

That brought a laugh from everyone except Willie.

They left the yard in a tight group until they reached the place where Romeo was attacked. Matt got down and started working at following the tracks where they left the area. After about a hundred yards he knew the general direction they were headed. There were no other tracks to interfere, and he had no trouble following them from horseback.

The tracks merged into an old cattle trail down to the river. They left a good trail where they came out of the river on the other side, and the pace was picked up. Matt was traveling at a fast trot and the rest of the group was fifty feet back.

After thirty minutes of riding Matt suddenly held up his hand to signal them to stop. Matt sat still listening for a long time while the group waited. Finally, Matt turned his horse and quietly rode back to meet them. He whispered, "I hear someone talking up there." He dismounted and handed his reins to John, "Hold my horse while I check it out."

He had just handed his reins to John when they heard a slight crashing sound coming from the brush just off to their left. It was too loud to be someone trying to sneak up on them, but too quiet to be a casual traveler going about his business.

Everyone drew their sidearms and eased down off their horses. Each man put his hand on his horse's nose to keep them quiet.

The slight noise stopped and then started again. Tension ran high as they waited. Then there was a slight whimper like an animal in pain and more noise from the brush. Then everything was silent for a long time. Lefty motioned for Matt to follow him and they eased into the brush toward where they last heard the noise. When they had gone thirty feet or so, Clay motioned for Luke to follow him, and they followed Matt and Lefty. They only went another twenty-five feet when they discovered the source of the noise. Lefty rushed forward while Matt stood with his gun ready. The man was lying with his face in the dirt and when Lefty rolled him over and saw his face he almost threw up. Lefty whispered, "Oh my God, it's Romeo."

Before they attempted to move him, they checked him for wounds and found cuts and bruises all over his body. It looked as if he had been beaten almost to death. Both eyes were black and swollen almost closed, his lips were cut and swollen to twice their normal size and there was blood all over him.

"What in the world did they do to you, Romeo?"

Romeo looked up into Lefty's eyes, clutched his hand, and whispered, "They beat me Lefty, they beat me, but I didn't tell them anything. They just beat me some more. I'm all broke up inside, I can feel it. It hurts, Lefty, it hurts."

"Ok, you just be quiet for now. We're gonna take you home. They are not gonna hurt you anymore, we got you now, you just rest easy."

Clay and Luke arrived and heard the last part of what Romeo said.

Clay turned to Luke and Matt, "He can't ride like that, we'll have to make a travois. See if anyone has something to cut some poles, or maybe there are some downed trees we can use."

Matt hurried back to the rest of the group to get them started gathering the material they would need.

They had momentarily forgotten about the voices Matt heard until there was a shout from that direction followed by more shouts and cursing. Someone yelled "Get out there and find him! Don't come back without him!"

The brush and timber came alive with people thrashing through making enough noise to wake the dead.

Clay and his men spread out and hid in the brush waiting for the searchers to come to them.

One by one, as they stumbled upon one of Clay's men they were overpowered, tied, and gagged. When they counted five men tied up lying in a row, Clay said, "Ok, let's go get the rest of them."

Silently, and slowly, they advanced on what they assumed was the camp of the outlaws. Three men were standing around a small fire waiting for their men to come back with their prisoner. They were not being very alert, since they were not expecting anyone else to be in the area.

Clay, Luke, Matt, and John were crouched in the brush within hearing distance of the camp, and their presence was still not known. As Clay watched, he recognized the man shouting the orders as none other than Carl Krauss.

After watching a few more minutes, to be sure there were no other men about that they had not seen, Clay whispered to Luke, "Cover me." He waited until Krauss had his back to him, and then stood and started walking toward him with his revolver in his hand pointed down by his side. He was hoping Krauss would go for his gun so he could end this now. When Krauss turned around and saw Clay he was only twenty feet away. Carl was so startled he staggered back two steps before he caught his balance, "Where the hell did you come from?"

"From your worst nightmare, Carl."

The other two men whirled around when they heard Clay's voice. One of them went for his gun and three shots, sounding as one, rang out. The man staggered back and fell to the ground groaning and holding his chest. The other one was in shock and didn't move.

Clay waited to see what Carl was going to do.

When he just stood there staring at him, Clay asked him, "We'll, are you gonna pull that gun, or you just gonna stare me to death?"

Carl was stammering trying to say something but nothing was coming out.

"If you're not gonna use it then drop it. We're gonna take you back to town and lock you up until the circuit judge comes through, and then we are gonna try you for murder, and with any luck, we will hang you by the neck until you are dead."

Krauss looked like he couldn't make up his mind, so Clay asked Luke to take his gun and tie him.

When that was done, and they started back to their horses, Clay said to no one in particular, "See if there's an ax here that we can use to make a travois."

An ax was found, and a travois was ready in no time. They used a blanket to cover the poles, and Romeo was strapped to it.

Three men lifted Romeo to put him on the travois. Two had his arms, and one had his feet. When they started lifting he screamed and passed out. They thought he was dead until they laid him on the travois and saw he was still breathing and had a pulse, so it must have been the pain that caused him to faint.

Matt and Lefty were overseeing the job of getting Romeo home safely while the rest of the men were riding herd on the captives.

When they reached the road leading to Cuero, Clay instructed Luke and the rest of his men to take the prisoners to jail and send the doctor out as soon as he can get here.

When they arrived home with Romeo, Marilyn and Alice came running out wanting to know what happened.

Romeo was put to bed in the guest room in the house and made as comfortable as they could get him. He was in terrible pain, and all he could do was groan. If he tried to move at all he screamed and murmured, "No, no, no more, please, no more."

Marilyn and Alice worked over him for an hour cleaning the blood off and putting ointment on his cuts. He finally drifted off in an uneasy sleep. They watched over him until the doctor arrived just before dark. He felt and poked around all over Romeo and finally said, "I think he probably has several broken ribs, numerous lacerations, and bruises, but the worst thing may be internal injuries, and I can't tell if there are or not. If he starts spitting or passing blood in his urine or bowels, then we will know, but there's probably nothing I can do about it, so let's hope that doesn't happen. In the meantime, just keep him quiet, give him warm soup and broth if he wants it. But don't let him get out of bed until we know if he has internal injuries.

He left a large bottle of pain medicine to be used as needed and said he would check on him again in a couple of days. "If he takes a turn for the worse, send someone for me."

The men returned from town just as the doctor was leaving and wanted to know how Romeo was. They got the same report as the others. One by one they came in to check on him and offered to sit with him during the night. Marilyn and Alice thanked them but assured them they had it covered. They would take turns watching over him. If they needed anything they would send for them.

CHAPTER SEVENTEEN

arl Krauss was transferred to Victoria for trial since the crimes he was accused of were committed in Victoria County. That wasn't as convenient as it would have been if he could be tried in DeWitt County, but that's the way things turned out.

Alice finally got to file for divorce. It was granted on the first hearing when the judge heard all the charges filed against Carl.

She left the courthouse smiling and accompanied Willie, Clay, Marilyn and their two children to the café for a big lunch followed up with ice cream for the kids.

Willie and Alice then went to the bank, and back to the courthouse, and changed all the records to remove Carl's name from all records having anything to do with the ranch and Alice.

As they left the courthouse Alice had tears of happiness streaming down her face. "Oh what a relief, I feel like a tremendous weight has been lifted off me. I can actually breathe, can you believe it, Willie? I'm finally free." She stopped right there on the main street, grabbed him around the neck, kissed him on the lips, and hugged him so tightly he thought she would never let go, but he wasn't complaining. People stopped to stare at them, some laughed, some old women turned up their noses and said, "How disgusting, right here in front of everyone."

Alice and Willie just laughed and went on down the street arm in arm.

They went back to the café and ordered coffee and apple pie. When it came they took their time eating. Afterward, Willie asked her what she intended to do with her ranch. "What do you mean, what am I going to do with it?"

"I mean are you going to sell it, keep it, or what?"

Alice was taken aback for a moment, "I don't know, I haven't given it any thought. This has all happened so suddenly. What would you suggest?"

"I suggest you sell it and move in with me. After all, husband and wife should live together, don't you think?"

Alice's mouth dropped open and her hand covered it, her eyes got big and she started to shake all over. "Willie, are you, are you asking me to marry you?"

"Yes, I guess I am, will you marry me?"

"Yes, yes I'll marry you!"

There were only a few other people in the café and they all heard. When she said yes they cheered and clapped. The happy couple was embarrassed because they didn't even realize anyone else was around.

When they returned to the Bar W and everyone got the news Marilyn started planning. The wedding would take place next Saturday night right here at the Bar W and everyone was invited.

Carl Krauss trial came off as scheduled. He was found guilty of embezzlement, kidnapping, attempted murder and sentenced to fifty years in prison. Since he was already in his fifties he would probably die there.

The rest of the men with him when Romeo was kidnapped were found guilty of kidnapping and sentenced to five years each.

Romeo recovered slowly after an extended period of being bedridden.

The day of the wedding came and went without a hitch. The party lasted most of the night, and no one was moving when the sun came up the next morning.

A crew from the Bar W went with Alice and Willie to her ranch to round up all the livestock and drive them to market. With the money she received from their sale, she bought more property adjacent to that already owned by Willie. The way the properties were situated the group of Clay, Luke, Willie, and Ed now controlled over ten thousand acres of land. They still rounded up cattle from the free-range to add to theirs and drove them to the railhead at Abilene every spring.

Alice used part of her money to furnish the house Willie already had built. She made some changes, added a couple of rooms for the children she expected to fill them with.

Willie was just standing back shaking his head and watching her reshape his life.

When things looked like they couldn't get any better a group of horsemen rode up to the front of Willie and Alice's house. Alice was home alone at the time and didn't recognize any of them, but assuming they were friends of Willie's, she opened the door and stepped out onto the front porch. "Hello gentlemen, can I help y'all with something?"

"Are you the former Alice Taylor?"

Cold chills ran up and down her spine. A sinking feeling of doom overtook her. She had to grab the door frame to keep from falling.

She looked the men over again but didn't know any of them.

Tentatively she said she was. "What is this about?"

"We are kin of your former husband Carl, and we've come to collect what's ours."

"My former husband, as you put it, has no claim on anything here, now I will thank you for leaving this instant."

"We are not leaving until we get what's ours."

"And just what is it that you think is yours?"

"Half the cattle you sold belonged to Carl, so we want the money he is due for his half."

"I don't have any money here, so I couldn't give it to you if I wanted to, which I don't, and even if I did, I would never give you one cent after what he did to me. Now get off this property."

She turned and went into the house and reached for the shotgun over the door. Before she could bring it down the door flew open and men stormed in, pushed her to the floor, took the shotgun, broke it open and removed the shells, and threw them on the floor beside her. Every time she attempted to get to her feet someone pushed her back down. One of them told her, "Just stay there and you won't get hurt."

She scooted back until her back was resting against the wall. She was frightened almost to the point of fainting thinking about what they might do to her. Then she thought about Willie who was due home at any moment, and her fear doubled thinking what they would do to him.

They went through the house, opened every drawer and cabinet, dumped the contents on the floor, broke the dishes, and destroyed everything she had just built. The new furniture was turned over, broken, and piled in a corner.

Alice was horrified at the destruction. When they had done all the damage they could do inside they went outside and started on the barns and fences. Fence posts were ripped out of the ground and thrown in a pile and set fire. The poles from the fences were added to the fire and soon a huge black smoke was reaching to the sky.

Willie was riding toward the house when he saw the smoke. At first, he couldn't make out where it was coming from, but as soon as he realized it was coming from his place, he put the spurs to his horse and raced as fast as he could go until he was close enough to see the group of horses standing in front of the house. With that many horses there he knew there were more men than he could handle alone, so he whipped in behind a mesquite bush to get a better perspective of what was going on before he went storming in there and got himself killed. He saw men tearing his fences down and burning them while others prowled around the house with guns. He knew it was a death trap if he rode in there now.

Alice was there, but there was nothing he could do to help her unless he had help. He turned his horse and raced as fast as he could to the Bar W headquarters. He had just left there so he knew most of the men would be there ready to eat their supper.

He stormed into the barnyard screaming to get their attention. Men came running from all directions with their guns in their hands. He briefly explained what was going on. The words were no more out of his mouth before horses were being caught and guns were grabbed. Most of the men mounted without the benefit of a saddle and someone yelled, "Let's go!" and the race was on. When they reached Willie's place the men were all gone but the fire was still raging. Willie raced into the house yelling Alice's name. He found her still crumpled in the corner in total shock.

He grabbed her by the shoulders and lifted her, "Alice, did they hurt you, I'll kill every one of them? Are you ok?"

When Alice realized it was Willie, she grabbed him and hung on, sobbing and shaking. Willie kept asking if she was hurt. She finally shook her head and said she was not hurt, just scared.

He hugged her and held her until she stopped shaking. He got her a cup of water and told her to drink it. She did and slowly composed herself, and told him what happened, and who the men were.

"Ok, you sit here and relax, everything is ok now. The men are gone, you're not hurt, and everything else can be fixed."

Clay and the rest of the men walked around looking at the damage. Some whistled, some shook their heads, some cussed a blue streak, but all promised to get the men who did this.

Clay went outside and told the men without saddles to get saddled up, bring all your guns and ammunition, we have some riding to do. The race was on back to the barn to get saddles and guns. It only took about thirty minutes before they were all ready to ride.

The trail led off in a direct line toward Meyersville. "They've got to be more relatives of Mr. Krauss. Maybe we can clean out that whole nest of snakes this time."

Every man in the group had blood in their eyes as they followed the trail. It was still so fresh they smelled the dust in the air.

After a few minutes of wild riding, Clay slowed them down to warn them of a possible ambush. "We are so close behind them they could stop and kill half of us before we knew what hit us. Let's hang back and follow them until they stop, and then we can put the screws to them."

"Yeah, they will probably go to a saloon somewhere to celebrate." Luke offered, "If they do, we'll have the whole bunch in one place."

Matt was sent on ahead as a scout to keep all of them from riding into an ambush. The rest of the group was fifty yards back, but close enough that they could see Matt if he ran into trouble.

It was about twenty miles from the Bar W to the town of Meyersville. The trip took close to four hours and was fully dark long before the group reached the town.

Matt and Clay rode in alone while the rest of their men waited at the edge of town. They didn't want to set off an alarm by all of them riding in together.

They rode slowly down the street like any two cowboys coming to town for a drink until they reached the first saloon.

Clay and Matt looked at each other and nodded, pulled their horses over to the hitch rail, and dismounted. Matt held their horses while Clay inspected the group of horses tied up in front.

He approached the first horse and ran his hand over its flank. It came away wet, so he went to each of the other horses and found the same thing. All of those horses were ridden hard and arrived here in the last few minutes. He returned to Matt and said, "This is it. That's their horses. They must all be inside. Ride back and get the men, come in quietly and tie up across the street. Half of you cover the back, the other half come to the front with me.

There were seven men in Clay's bunch, so three went to cover the back of the saloon, and three came to meet Clay outside the front door.

At the prearranged signal they all entered at the same time with guns drawn. They spread out along the front and back walls and Clay got their attention by firing a shot into the ceiling.

"Don't anyone move unless you want to die. I'm Clay Wade and these are all friends of mine. We want the six men riding the horses tied up out front, and we want them now. If you did not ride in here the last ten minutes or so, get up and stand against that wall, and keep your hands away from your guns. We don't want you."

Several men slowly got to their feet with their hands in the air and moved to the wall. Six men were left sitting, all looked like a kid who got caught with his hand in the cookie jar.

"We'll, we'll, we'll. That looks like y'all are going to be the main attraction at our party. I'm sorry we didn't bring you any party hats, but we do have a tie for you. It may get a little snug around your neck, but I'm sure you will regret your evening's activities before it's over. Now, I want each of you to slowly stand, one at a time, and drop your gun belt, starting with you." He pointed at the man closest to him. "Just so you understand, you will make me very happy if you decide not to follow my orders. After what y'all did today nothing that happens to you will make any of us lose any sleep tonight. And, you see that man right there? It was his house you ransacked, and his wife that you almost scared to death. So if he suddenly takes a notion to extract some blood and guts as payment, none of us are going to stop him."

He wiggled his gun to indicate the man should stand and drop his gun.

After a few seconds of hesitation, during which time Clay, and at least one other, clicked the hammers back on their revolvers. The sound of the cylinders turning sounded like a hammer on steel. The man stood and dropped his gun belt and sat back down. Clay stepped forward and kicked the gun to the middle of the floor and pointed to the next man. "Your turn, drop it."

Each man took his turn going through the drill until they all were unarmed.

Clay turned to the men lined up against the wall, "Do any of you have any connection to these men?"

When no one answered, he asked if any of them were related. Again he got no answer. "Ok, take a seat at those two tables over there, but keep your hands away from your guns. It would be a big embarrassment if we misunderstood your actions and shot you by mistake."

When everything was quiet in the room, Clay walked around looking at each of the men. He saw one that had a strong resemblance to Carl Krauss. Clay stopped in front of him and stared for the longest time. The man began to sweat and looked down at the floor.

After a few more minutes of letting the man sweat, Clay asked him, "I'm going to guess that you are Carl's brother. Am I right?"

The man looked up at Clay and then quickly back at the floor, but didn't answer.

Clay waited a few seconds, and then hooked his toe under the front of the man's chair and slapped his open palm to the man's forehead, and shoved. The man and chair toppled over backward. His head hit the floor with a splat. It sounded like a watermelon popping open. The man grabbed his head and rolled to his side, moaning. He rolled back and forth a few times before he stopped and lay still. Clay turned to the next man who also could have been related to Carl, and asked him, "Is he Carl's brother?" The man didn't move or say anything. Clay gave him a few seconds to answer and when he still had not answered Clay took a step toward him, the man held up his hands, and said, "Yes, they are brothers."

"And what is your relation to Carl?"

"I'm his brother too."

"Oh, so this is a family affair. Do y'all always commit your crimes together?"

When there was no answer, Clay asked, "Who else is related to Carl Krauss?"

No one answered. Clay walked around the room looking at each man as he did so.

With no warning, and so suddenly that everyone in the room jumped, Clay drew his revolver and fired a shot into the ceiling. He shouted, "I want answers! Who else is related to Carl Krauss?"

Three of the men threw up their hands.

Clay walked to the first one, "What is your relation to Carl?"

"He's my wife's cousin."

He moved to the next one, "What is your relation to Carl?"

"He's my uncle."

"And you other men who are not related, why are you riding with them to do their dirty work?"

Again no one wanted to answer. Clay had holstered his gun, but when he got no answer, he quickly drew it again and pulled the hammer back.

"Alright, I'll tell you." One of the men spoke up, "We've been doing some jobs off and on for Carl and his brothers. They asked us if we wanted to have some fun, so we went along. We didn't know there was going to be a woman involved and burning, and stuff like that."

"So, what do you think we should do with you? You ransack a mans home, you scare his wife half to death, you tear his fences down and burn them. What is a fitting punishment for men who do that? What would you want to do if someone did that to you? You first, what would you do?"

The man he pointed to was Carl's nephew. The man looked surprised and shook his head, "I don't know, I'd probably want to kill him."

"Do you think we should kill you?"

"No, I didn't mean that, I meant I'd probably want to, but I wouldn't do it."

"Oh, it's a different punishment if you do it. Is that right?"

The man had no answer. All was quiet while they thought about it.

Finally, Clay asked, "This is Gonzales County, right?"

One of the men shook his head yes.

"I happen to be friends with the sheriff of Gonzales County. I think we'll just haul y'all up there and tell him what y'all did and get his opinion. What do you think about that?"

Carl's brother had been listening to the conversation from his position on the floor. He rolled over and sat up. Still holding his head, he slowly got to his feet. "Look Wade, maybe we went a little too far. How about we pay the man for his trouble and call it even?"

"I don't think you have enough money to pay for what y'all did. No, I think a judge will have to decide the best punishment for all of you. Let's get them loaded up boys. We should be able to make Gonzales by mid-morning if we don't have to stop to bury anybody. On your feet, let's go."

When the men were mounted their hands were tied to the horn and their feet tied together under the horse.

It was midmorning the next day when the procession rode down the main street of Gonzales. By the time they reached the jail the sidewalks were lined with people wondering what was going on. The men's feet were untied and they were marched into the sheriff's office. When the door opened and Clay stepped back to let the prisoners in, the sheriff stood up from behind his desk and watched as Clay lined them up along the wall. Their hands were still tied so it was obvious they were charged with some crime.

When everyone was finally inside, the room was packed from wall to wall.

The Sheriff had not said a word until Clay closed the door and turned to face him.

"Sheriff, I'm Clay Wade, these are friends of mine, and those over there are not. This is Mr. Stanton. Those men broke into Mr. Stanton's home, scared his wife half to death, ransacked his house and barn, tore down all his corral fences and burned them, all because they claimed, without an ounce of proof, I might add, that Mr. Stanton's wife owed them money. When she didn't have the money they claimed she owed them, they destroyed their home. So what do you think we should do with them?"

"Why didn't you just shoot 'em and save us all a lot of trouble?"

"Believe me, Sheriff, we thought about it."

"Since you brought 'em here I'll have to lock 'em up and let the judge decide what to do with 'em."

"Do you know when the judge will be able to hear the case?"

"Nope, he has a lot of territories to cover, so we never know when he'll make it around to us. I'll have to let you know. How will we get in touch with you?"

You can send a telegram to the sheriff in Cuero. He's pretty good about getting messages to us. But we'll need a day or two notice to get here."

"That shouldn't be a problem."

The prisoners were herded into a couple of cells, and Clay and his men went to the first eating joint and enjoyed a good meal. It was the first one since noon yesterday.

It was late that day when they reached the Bar W. Everyone was exhausted, and after a quick meal, went straight to bed.

A week later a message came that the trials for the Krauss gang would start on Monday. That was four days away, so the Wade bunch had plenty of time. They planned to get there a day early to sit down with the prosecutor to discuss the case. With Alice, Willie, and Clay to testify against them, the crooks didn't stand much of a chance, but you never know what a defense attorney will come up with.

When the prosecutor read the statement to the jury, they stared at the gang, and you could tell their verdict was not going to be favorable to the crooks.

They shouldn't have been worried, because the defense attorney wasn't much of an attorney and offered very little defense. All were found guilty and sentenced to a minimum of ten years in prison.

When the sentence was handed down by the judge, the defendants jumped to their feet and attacked the judge's bench. The one bailiff on duty and the deputy sheriff were overpowered and stripped of their guns. The courtroom was full, and people were scrambling to get out the door. Chairs and benches were overturned, dragged out the door and down the steps. Those who were unlucky enough to fall during the stampede were trampled by those behind them. It was total mayhem, with women screaming, shots fired, and no one in control. The outlaws were now armed and dangerous and looking for targets.

When the men first jumped to their feet and attacked the bailiff, Clay and Willie grabbed Alice and pushed her to the floor hoping to keep her out of sight. One of the men spotted Clay and aimed, but before he could pull the trigger Clay shot him in the face. He screamed and fell back with blood streaming from the hole just below his right eye.

The prisoners were shooting mostly to keep the people's heads down while they escaped out the back door.

Clay and Willie emptied their guns at them as they scrambled to escape. Several of them fell, but of those who were able to make it out the door, some were injured. Finally, the courtroom was empty and Alice was lifted from the floor unhurt.

Clay ran to check on the deputy, the bailiff, and the judge. The judge was fine, but the bailiff and deputy were wounded but appeared to have non-life-threatening injuries.

Just as things were quieting down the sheriff came running through the door with his gun drawn. "What in the world happened here?"

Clay explained with as few words as possible and the sheriff called for volunteers to join the posse to go after the escapees. There was no shortage of men offering to join, and they were gone in a cloud of dust in fifteen minutes.

Four men were lying wounded, or dead, just outside the back door of the courthouse. They never made it to the horses that someone had waiting for them. Two men escaped, but from the blood trail leading to where the horses waited, they probably would not go far.

An hour after the posse left, they returned with two bodies across their saddles. All six were accounted for and only two were able to return to their jail cell to be held until they were healthy enough to be transported to Huntsville prison.

Rather than make the long trip home so late in the day, rooms were taken at the hotel for the night. After a good meal, Willie and Alice slipped away and headed for their room. When the door was closed and locked Alice turned to Willie, wrapped her arms around his neck, and gave him a long, sweet kiss.

"Since that dirty business is finished, what do you say we start a family, right now."

He had no verbal response.

THE END

If you enjoyed reading this book please look up other books written by Art Clepper.

BOOKS BY ART CLEPPER

LONG TRAIL TO TEXAS

REVENGE TEXAS STYLE

THE LOST MAN